Promises Under Fire

DEANN KRUEMPEL

COPYRIGHT INFORMATION

Promises Under Fire
First published in United States by BookStudio
2741 Kraft Lane, Missouri Valley, Iowa 51555

www.mybookstudio.com

Text Copyright © DeAnn Kruempel 2020

Cover image by DeAnn Kruempel
Text and layout by BookStudio

Paperback ISBN: 9781952891045

CONTENTS

"Do small things
With great love."
Mother Teresa

Promises to Keep Series

Promises to Keep

Promises Challenged

Promises Strengthened

Promises in Courage

Promises Under Fire

Dedicated to Billie, who is now preparing the banquet tables of heaven, setting up the daily entertainment and making sure all are properly attired.

Thank you for everything!

Promises Under Fire

NOVEMBER 2, 1941

Does life just seem different when one turns fourteen or have things changed that much?

My struggle with polio was a challenge for everyone in the family, but now Mom says she can barely detect a limp when I walk. Having experienced this dreadful disease, hopefully I will have more empathy for my patients someday when I am a doctor. My dream! Every year I get that much closer to accomplishing it. On weekends and during the summer I have been helping Dr. Evans and his wife, Becky at his clinic in Canterbury, which also gives me insight into what it will be like to be a doctor.

Last year I cleaned house for a neighbor, Gertrude Niggle, when she was expecting a baby. The job was dreadful at first. Gert was very demanding and unkind, but later, when she feared losing her baby Laurene from whooping cough, the woman had a change of heart. She finally realized what was really important in life. Gert and Mort have a son, Lem. He was a bully at school until this year. Now he sits alone in the back row and talks very little.

Mom, Michael and I promised Dad before he died more than three years ago that we would not give up, no matter what happened in life. Mostly, we have kept the promise. Losing the only man she had ever loved, our mother grieved for a long time. She is stronger now and I think her heart is healing. Our home is filled with laughter once again. Mother is close friends with Lynn Swanson. She and her husband, Brad, publish the local newspaper. Brad hopes to publish a story and photographs in Life magazine.

Grandma lived with us until last year. She was our rock when Dad died and Mom withdrew into her grief. I don't know what we would have done without her. Last fall, she married William Harrison, neighbor and close friend. Now she lives just up the road with her husband and his brother, Geoffrey. We miss having Grandma here with us, but she is very happy in her new life. Though Geoffrey is often a prankster and teases her mercilessly, she loves him like a real brother.

Geoffrey and William are twins and have the innate ability to read each other's thoughts. They also have a special way with animals that is truly amazing. They have taught Michael about farming and animals. Now, it seems my brother also possesses that ability to communicate with nature's creatures.

11

I love school! Ethel is a wonderful teacher. This is our second year of remembering to address her as "Miss Bollinger" instead of Ethel. She took over when Miss Johnston married Greg Christle- ton, and became Vicky and Ricky's mommy.

Mabel, Julia, and Lilly Svenson, Ethel and I have wonderful talks during lunch at school. It is good to have friends who help us through hard times and encourage each other's dreams.

A letter finally arrived from Ethel's cousin, Billie, who has become my dear friend, too. Her family moved from Boulder to get away from the violence at her father's coal mine. He and his friends found a job in a mine in a different town, Oak Creek, Colorado. Billie and her sister, Dru, have become close friends with two Japanese girls, whose father is also a coal miner. I am so glad they are all safe and happy in their new home.

Mom says I am too young to have a beau. I have never thought much about it until lately. Every day I look forward to seeing Benjamin Hindricks at school. Sometimes I look up to see him looking at me, which is embarrassing. I know I blush, but it also makes my heart sing. He is kind, thoughtful, smart and very handsome! Now we are just friends, but a girl can dream...

In spite of love of family and strong friendships, something formidable is lurking in the future. I can feel it. People are on edge, as if waiting for bad news. At Bellum's store the men who gather around the stove to talk become silent the minute I walk in. Dear friend and neighbor, Geoffrey, says that our country cannot stay out of the war in Europe much longer. Then I see him glance at Michael with sadness in his eyes and shake his head. Hitler's army is sweeping into more countries. Radio newscasts report daily of the atrocities committed against the Jews and others Hitler hates. Americans remember the Great Depression just a few years ago and the Dust Bowl, when it did not rain for years and there were no crops to harvest. People were hungry and poor and now worry that war will bring about the same hardships. When the radio news reporters speak of fighting and death, we can change the station, but that does not stop the scary part, it only prevents us from hearing it. That can only go on for so long.

I wonder what the future will bring. —L.A.

CHAPTER 1

SO, IT BEGINS

Something was dreadfully wrong. Mabel and Julia stepped inside the porch door and stopped, taking it all in. The problem was not with what they heard or saw, but with what was missing. No clanking of a kettle cover as it was lifted to test the potatoes. No smell of seasoned meatloaf sizzling in the oven. No rattle of silverware as it was placed on the supper table. In the background from the shelf in the living room, they could hear the radio blaring. The voice of the announcer grew louder and then faded in a haze of static. He was shouting frantically something about Pearl Harbor, but the roaring noise of airplanes in the background smothered bits of his message.

Then they heard it. The sound of sobbing. Wretched, convulsive weeping coming from the kitchen. The two rushed in, not bothering to un-buckle their manure-and-snow-crusted chore boots.

"Ma! Ma, what is the matter?" Mabel reached her first and placed her hand on her shoulder, but their mother's face was buried in her arms that lay crossed on the table in front of her. The folds of her sweater muffled her sobs, but her whole body shud-dered with agony. The girls pulled chairs in and sat, holding their mother close, wondering what dread-ful event had occurred. At last, the woman lifted her head. She drew in a deep breath and looked at each of her daughters with red, swollen eyes.

She shook her head slowly, her shoulders slumped in devastation. "Now, there is war." She paused for a few seconds, then her features again contorted in pain. "And I have four boys!" With a heart-wrenching wail, her face fell back to her arms.

CHAPTER 2

SCHOOL DAZE

For the first time in her brief career as a school teacher, Ethel did not need to ring the bell to call the students inside for class. She sat, hands folded on her desk, and greeted each child with what she hoped was a calm, reassuring smile. They shuffled in slowly, sank into their desks and then looked up at her with frightened eyes. Even the youthful eagerness of Ricky and Vicky, the first grade Christleton twins, had been replaced with frowns of uncertainty. The attack on Pearl Harbor had changed everything. Was this another casualty of war, the teacher wondered, the loss of childhood laughter and the sheer joy of being alive?

Entering quietly, Lilly, Julia, Mabel and Emma Svenson glanced at the other students as they approached their teacher's desk. "Sorry we are late, Miss Bollinger. We had extra chores." They did not mention that their ma, distressed that she would lose her sons to the war, refused to leave her bed that morning so there was no breakfast and no lunch pails packed for them.

At last, all 22 students waited expectantly in their one-room school house. No one spoke, and there was an uneasiness in the air that bruised the silence. Boots scraped faintly on the rough wooden floor. Giant breaths of air were sucked in unconsciously and held, worry and uncertainty banked inside like thunderheads ready to burst.

Staring out at the children whose lives and education had been entrusted to her, Ethel felt a sudden surge of panic. They were frightened and unsure of the future and waiting for her guidance. The teacher's heart pounded like a hammer in her chest. Should she dismiss school for the day? For the week? Surely, it was the parents' job to comfort their children at times such as this. What was it they needed? Could she give it to them?

Her eyes met those of children she had grown to love in the past year. She breathed a silent prayer, and a gentle smile lit her face as she suddenly knew what needed to be done.

"Students, let us stand for the Pledge of Allegiance." Tensions eased as they scrambled to their feet and spoke the same words in unison that they said every school day.

We can take a few minutes each morning to talk about the war or any worries that you may have. Do you have questions today?"

Emma Svenson raised her hand hesitantly, for she had not dared ask at home. "Teacher, do you think that the war will happen here? Will the Japanese drop bombs on Iowa, like they did at Pearl Harbor?"

After giving an answer she hoped would reassure the children, the young woman continued with the daily class routine, but Miss Ethel Bollinger knew in her heart that from this day on, her classroom would never be the same.

CHAPTER 3

UNCLE SAM WANTS YOU!

The wind-carved waves of white stretched far into the fields like ripples in an endless ocean. Michael noticed a black spattering of dirt crusted on the northern side of every small hill. Harsh winds had snatched up bits of exposed soil and slammed them into the tiny drifts making them smudged and tainted. It was as though the war had even ravaged the beauty of the snow.

Normally on these short drives to Canterbury, Geoffrey regaled Michael with tales of his growing up years in northern England where he and William had lived with their mother on a small farm. Mischief would dance in Geoffrey's eyes when he made the young boy giggle, delighted with the stories. This drive was not the same.

Today Geoffrey drove in silence, and Michael wondered if it had been a good idea to ask the dear old neighbor to take him to Canterbury to do Christmas shopping. Michael had finished wood carvings: a tiny sewing machine for Grandma, a teacup for Mom and a doctor bag for Lydi, but he hoped to find something at the store for Grandpa William and for Geoffrey. The two old gentlemen had taken the boy under their wings since his father died and encouraged his dream to be a farmer. They had given him Dottie, his first sheep. Michael loved the old men dearly.

Finally, the man and boy arrived in Canterbury and parked the old pickup outside Chet Bellum's mercantile. Entering the store, they noticed several colorful, new posters taped up in the windows. Michael slowed his pace so he could read them. There was a large picture of Uncle Sam proudly carrying an eagle on his outstretched arm. Printed in huge letters at the top were the words, "Defend your country! Enlist now in the U.S. Army!" On another, an evil-looking Japanese soldier pointed a gun right at Michael as he stared at the poster. "He is the enemy," was penned in a large arrow pointing at the soldier. Another flashy banner displayed a cheerful painting of a family gathered around the table passing platters of turkey and bowls of mashed potatoes and vegetables. The caption read: "Ours to fight for. Freedom from Fear. Freedom from Want."

Inside, where the store shared the post office, more posters were taped on the doors. On one, an arm wrapped with a swastika band, the symbol of Hitler's army, had thrust a huge knife through a Bible. Michael's stomach twisted at the thought.

Geoffrey visited with Chet for a few minutes. The store owner commented on how fast the government got the posters printed and sent out. "Yup, they want everybody to join up," he said. "It'll sure take lots of man power to win the war." Michael thought the man was about to say more, but with a downward glance at him, Mr. Bellum gave Geoffrey a knowing look. What did Grandma say when children were not supposed to hear what was said? *There are ears in the cornfield?*

Michael browsed through the store. He found a jack knife he thought William could use for tree grafting and a shiny new fountain pen for Geoffrey and made his purchase with Mr. Bellum. When he turned to the door he saw Geoffrey staring at another of the posters. In huge red letters across the top was the word WARNING! In the center was a photo of a little boy and girl being tucked into bed by their parents. Peering over their shoulders was a Japanese soldier with a gun. "Our homes are in danger!" was stamped across the bed.

"Are you ready to go home?" Michael looked up at his dear friend who was lost in thought.

"Hm?" Geoffrey responded absently, his eyes remaining glued to the picture. Finally, he felt Michael tugging on his arm. "Oh, have you finished your shopping already, lad?"

The man and the boy rode home in silence.

"I will walk home from your place," Michael told Geoffrey as they pulled into the man's driveway. "That way I can talk to Grandpa William and Grandma for a while. I miss her since she and William got married."

Geoffrey immediately slipped away into the living room and soon the sound of a radio newscast hummed in the background. The young boy told his grandpa and grandma about the war posters at the store. William frowned and shook his head. "Propaganda. Our government did not waste any time circulating war materials." He rested his hand on his grandson's shoulder. "The purpose of propaganda is to manipulate people, to get them to do and feel what the government wants."

Michael pondered his grandfather's words for a moment. "Well, I think that propaganda stuff is working." The older man simply listened. "Mom says I shouldn't hate anybody, but I kind of hate those Jap guys." The boy's head dropped as he added in a quiet voice, "And I'm only nine, but I feel sad that I can't join up and go fight."

Chuckling softly, the man ruffled his grandson's blond hair. "As you grow older and wiser, lad, you will learn to sort out the facts, decide what is important, and then make intelligent choices. Now, let's get you home before your mum wonders what happened to you!"

CHAPTER 4

REJECTION

Two hairy tails whipped his legs wildly as Geoffrey entered the front porch. He stooped to pat Romeo and Juliet on their silky black and white heads. Romeo whined softly and licked his hand. "I'm all right, boy." The farmer managed a weak smile, knowing that the dogs sensed human emotions better than humans did. The border collies had been part of the family for more than seven years. They were partial to him, he thought, and they seemed to know what he was feeling. If the weather had been warmer, he would have sat down right there in the wooden rocker on the porch and he knew he'd have good company. No, it was cold, and besides, he might as well get this over with.

Geoffrey stepped inside, hung his gray wool coat on the hall tree and pulled off his leather boots. A glance at his gold pocket watch told him it was tea time. William and Christina would be enjoying the winter luxury of afternoon tea. He padded slowly to the kitchen, pulled out a chair and sank down with a heavy sigh. Then he slid a large brown envelope onto the table in front of William. His shoulders slouched with the weight of the world as he stared at the ceramic teapot.

William's eyes met his wife's over his wire-rimmed spectacles. She stood and went to put water on the stove for another pot of tea. The old gentleman folded the newspaper he had been reading and set his glasses on top of it. "Brother Geoffrey, do you wish to talk about what is on your mind?"

Silence ensued while the two brothers sat. Christina brought a cup and saucer from the cupboard and took the rose-patterned plate to the counter to add four more sugar cookies. Finally,

Geoffrey lifted his head and pointed at the envelope. "That was supposed to prove that I am fit to be a soldier." Christina drew in a breath of shock, but stood still, staring out the window toward the barn.

"So, you tried to enlist in the Army?" William spoke softly, gently, with a calm that he did not feel inside.

"Air Force. I fancied being a pilot. Navigating the incredible machines that can annihilate enemy planes and ships. I am certain I am still capable of such exploits!" Geoffrey's fist came down on the table so hard the cups rattled in their saucer nests. His face fell again to his chest. "But they do not want me."

"And where did you get this idea that you should join the Air Force?" William asked his brother with no malice in his voice.

"The news reports nearly every day describe Hitler's relentless bombing of our mother country.

Geoffrey, will there be anything left of England when they are finished? I scrutinized the posters that shout from every window in Canterbury. 'Enlist now. Your country needs you! Every real man wants to be a soldier!'" As though his dramatic recitation had drained him of all strength, his next words were raspy and weak, spoken in a whisper. "I feel guilty because I am too old to fight."

"That is precisely what is intended by the creators of the posters! Geoffrey, as you become older and wiser you will sift through the propaganda and discover the facts. Then you will be able to make wise choices."

Geoffrey shook his head in solemn agreement, ignoring the jibe about becoming older and wiser. "But I am already too old to be a soldier."

"A war is not fought only by soldiers, Geoffrey. What is accomplished on the home front is as critical to winning as tactics in battle." Their eyes met and they communicated silently in the ways common to twins. Geoffrey's face lit and the corners of his mouth turned up ever so slightly. He placed his hands together under the table and almost, but not quite, rubbed them together. *Ah, yes, there is much to be done!* Geoffrey thought, and reached for one of Christina's sugar cookies.

CHAPTER 5

ONE BY ONE

"They are gone. Arthur and Elmer left on the train yesterday for Camp Wheeler." Lilly reported to their friends as they sat at their desks during noon recess while frigid December winds howled outside the schoolhouse. She looked down at her folded hands. "Ma is beside herself with worry with two sons soon to be fighting in the war."

"Ja," her twin sister, Julia, added, recalling the night they had found their mother crying in the kitchen. "She is hoping the other two boys won't have to go. Pa says he doesn't think they will be drafted since they are needed to help on the farm. They may want to enlist like the other two, but Ma would have a fit. Guess it depends on how long the war goes on."

Mabel placed the cover on her lunch pail and brushed stray bread crumbs from her skirt. "Pa says us girls can do the chores and work in the fields. We always have, but there will be more work with fewer helpers. And, our sister Ida has a beau. She will marry soon. I don't know how much longer he'll let Lilly, Julia and I come to school." She sighed sadly.

"Will you manage all right without Elmer and Arthur?" Lydi asked softly. "Will your mother be all right?"

Julia nodded, though her head remained bowed. "We will all have to make it through. We have no other choice."

"Others are enlisting," said Mabel. "Arden and Amelia's mommy will have to take care of those little ones all by herself." Tears threatened to spill from her eyes as she met those of her friends.

"Some of these men will never come home." She could not help but wonder if their mother could bear the loss of a son, maybe more.

The four girls and their teacher friend sat in leaden silence. Today there was no sound of laughter or screaming children chasing through the playground or throwing snow in each other's faces. Like a giant tidal wave the war swept over all of them, seeping into their hearts and drowning every sigh of happiness, strangling the precious, innocent breath of youth.

The front door of the school squeaked as it opened and shut, followed by the sound of stomping feet. Emma entered the classroom and glanced at her three sisters and Lydi before taking her place at her desk. Soon Ricky and Vicky trampled in with wet snow still clinging to their boots. Their cheeks glowed pink, brushed by the raw winter wind.

Lydi took in each of the children there in Chaucer Township School Number Seven. Suddenly,

Grandpa William's words, what he had been pro-claiming since our country entered the war, streamed into Lydi's head. *What we do on the home front can help win the war.* Could they really make a difference?

With restored determination, Lydi stood and pulled her desk closer to her friends. Expectantly, they leaned toward her. Five young girls put their heads together. They whispered. Nodded. Scrib-bled small notes. Smiled. That day, at the Chaucer School noon recess, Project REACH was born.

CHAPTER 6

READY FOR CHRISTMAS

It was cookie baking day! Christina Harrison looked forward to spending time with Anna and the children. As she walked the half mile to her daughter's house, her heart overflowed with thankfulness. How many years has it been? There had been nothing left for her back in Sweden when her first husband had died, but she had been able to come to America with her daughter. Oh, times had been hard when Anna's man had died, but now she had her own family with dear William and his brother. And, she had Anna and two wonderful grandchildren. Today, they would fill coffee cans and gallon

jars with cookies for the holidays. Some of their fa-
vorites were recipes she had brought from Sweden,
ones she had made with her mother many years ago.

"Hi, Grandma! I'm ready to make cookies!
Mom says we're making the oatmeal ones first. I
get to grind the oatmeal and the raisins!" Young
Michael grinned broadly as he sat next to the
grinder, which was clamped to a small table in the
corner of the kitchen. It was made of heavy metal.
A crank with a wooden handle that turned an auger
was bolted onto the side. The auger pushed the food
through the blade and plate, which was simply a circle with small holes drilled throughout. A small
wingnut held the plate in place. The boy scooped
oatmeal into the funnel-like top and then turned the
crank. The oats came out in tiny particles and fell
into a glass bowl. When he finished the oats,
Grandma brought a carton of raisins, which made
the cranking much more difficult.

Grandma's raisin-filled oatmeal cookies were Lydi's favorite, a recipe the woman had brought from her mother in Sweden. The ground oatmeal was mixed with butter, eggs and flour, then rolled out into a thin layer. The children took turns cutting circles out of the dough while Grandma scooped them onto cookie sheets and started baking them. Anna stood at the cook stove, stirring the raisin filling. It was thick and sweet and could easily scorch.

Michael insisted it was youngest child's privilege to taste the batter and lick the spoon. His growing-boy hands were often caught snitching bits of dough, and they occasionally weaseled into the raisin box. Sometimes Grandma would scold and cuff his wrist with a teasing swat when she caught him, but tonight she smiled tolerantly at his antics. "Mae at the store said that Chet got word from his supplier that they are anticipating rationing. Each person will only be allowed to buy a small amount of some things." Grandma spoke as she and Lydi spooned raisin filling onto the crispy baked oatmeal discs. "It could be next year sugar will be rationed and we won't be making cookies."

Anna managed to pull both her children into a hug. "Yes, it could be Christmas will be very different next year. We may need to do without here in the states so that our soldiers will have enough."

Lydi loved baking with the family. The year she had polio she had missed it, so now she treasured the time even more. The thought of the war robbing them of special times wrenched at her heart. She recalled the plans the girls had made at school last week and had an idea. "Do you think we could share some of our Christmas baking with families whose sons or fathers or husbands have gone to fight? So many are afraid of what the war will bring. Christmas is not the same this year."

"I think that is a wonderful idea!" Anna said as she gave her daughter another quick hug. "We can make deliveries tomorrow when we go to town."

Michael found a scrap of paper and pencil and began to make a list as they each named families they thought would appreciate their gifts. Grandma pulled the fruitcake out of the pantry and began cutting thick slices. Lydi and her mother wrapped the baked goods in brown paper and tied each package with string, then carefully packed them into the large wicker basket. The girl looked forward to making the Christmas deliveries. It felt good to do something that might help families make it through this worrisome time.

CHAPTER 7

A WIFE AND CHILDREN

Lydi had never seen anything so elegant. Directly before them was the dining room table, a dark mahogany, with four tall matching chairs. A lovely chandelier made entirely of clear glass and crystal hung from the ceiling. The glass curved down at the top in an S shape and strands of crystals in various sizes draped down around each glass fixture, creating a tiny tinkling sound as a little girl and young boy bounced down the stairs.

"Mrs. Andersson, it is so nice to see you. And Lydi, who is such a help in Dr. Evans' office. This must be Michael, whom Arden has spoken of. Please come in." Mrs. Feldman greeted them graciously as her children scurried into place next to her. They waited politely, but fidgeted as though they could not wait to be unleashed. "You know Arden and Amelia," she said as she laid her hand on each child's shoulder.

Anna, Lydi and Michael stepped inside onto a rug that protected the gleaming hardwood floor. Anna thanked the woman and explained that they were visiting the homes that they knew had family members serving in the war.

"Well, you must stay for a bit. Arden has been waiting to have someone to play his new games. Truly, I would love some adult conversation. Please say you can come in. And I wish you would call me Grace." She smiled warmly.

"We can visit for a little while. Thank you, Grace." Anna answered as she bent down to remove her wet shoes. Michael hastily tugged off his boots, revealing his big toe, which was peeking out of a gaping hole in his socks. Anna closed her eyes in horror as the two boys bounded off to Arden's room. She peeped over at their hostess, desperately hoping she had not seen the hole. Obviously, it did not bother Michael.

Lydi held the tissue-wrapped package, but it did not seem as special as it had last night. Would these people even eat homemade goods? She could hardly take it back to the pickup. As Grace's face turned to Lydi, the girl held out the package. At once, warm hands surrounded hers. "Oh, I do hope there might be home-baked cookies in here!" She bent closer to sniff. "Fruitcake, too?" Lydi smiled and nodded, releasing a soft sigh of relief, as Grace carried the package to the table.

Amelia reached for Lydi's hand. "Come sit down and I will show you my dollies." Stocking feet sunk into thick carpets as all of the girls padded to the sitting room where a white couch, adorned with matching doilies on each arm, awaited them. Amelia scurried upstairs to her room. The women spoke of the weather and the church program on

Sunday while Lydi gazed around with wonder. A piano took up a large part of the room. It was not a tall, dark giant like those at school and church. It was flat and wide and a honey color. The curved top was propped open so one could see the insides. In the corner of the room, in the front windows stood a six-foot Christmas tree. Long, thin, lighted glass tubes were clipped to the branches. Bubbles magically floated to the top of each. Lydi counted twenty of the bubblers, but she wondered if she missed some because the tree was almost totally covered with glittering tinsel.

Mrs. Feldman's voice drifted into Lydi's focus. "Arden insisted on putting on tinsel for his father. At the end, it was being thrown on in handfuls." She shook her head as she looked at the tree. "I did not have the heart to remove some. Besides, it gives me something to write to Reginald. He will smile."

"Here are all my dollies." Amelia's arms were full as she bounced into the living room, struggling to keep from dropping one. She plopped them proudly onto Lydi's lap in a giant heap.

"They are beautiful, Amelia. Oh, my." She arranged them neatly on her skirt and counted. "Seven dollies. I bet they love to play with you. Shall we have a tea party?" Lydi and Amelia pretended to munch on cookies and drink from tiny cups. Amelia's giggles warmed the hearts of everyone in the room.

Anna noticed an open manila envelope on the coffee table in front of them. A black and white photo lay on top. Grace's gaze followed. "Reginald insisted that we have a family picture taken before he left." She sighed wistfully.

Suddenly, Arden and Michael burst into the room, each running to his own mother. Anna checked her watch, then announced that it was time for them to go. The Feldmans followed Anna and the children back to the entry. Anna thanked Grace and the children as they turned to go out the door.

The young mother held up the tissue package the family had brought. "These will be our Christmas Day treats," she said fondly. "Thank you for bringing such a special gift."

CHAPTER 8

A GRANDMOTHER

There was a narrow gap on the bottom step where part of the board had rotted away. The nail still protruded from the frame under the plank with nothing but a sliver in its hold. Paint was peeling from the wooden siding of the small house, which had bleached gray in the Iowa sun.

"Hey, look at that neat Christmas flag she's got!" Michael pointed to a colorful banner hanging in Sena Gullickson's front window. A blue star was sewn onto the center of a white background. A bright red four-inch strip framed the whole flag, which gleamed brightly from the inside of the glass.

"No, Michael, that is a Service Flag, and Sena will display it in her window as long as the war goes on. The blue star means that someone from this household is serving in the Armed Forces," Anna explained to her son as the family reached the door. Lydi hesitated before knocking, unsure of what they would encounter inside.

Soon they heard slow footsteps approaching, and a small white-haired lady opened the door. She peered out at her visitors for a few seconds before recognizing Lydi. "Well, it's Doc Evans' young helper! Did you bring your family to see me, girl?" Lydi introduced her mother and Michael. "My eyes don't work good anymore. I might just stop and see the doc about that next time I'm walkin' by his office. Well, you folks come on in for a spell."

The three followed Sena into a small front room. An old wooden rocking chair nestled next to a brown davenport. A woman's voice was singing from a Philco radio on the end table. The old woman reached for the knob to turn the sound down. "I sure do like that Dinah Shore music show.

Don't know what I'd do without my radio." She glanced at Michael as the three settled on the couch. "I bet you like to listen to baseball. That's my Levi's favorite. We used to listen to every Yankee game those summers before he joined the Marines." She stared at the one-starred flag in the window. "He was supposed to come home for Christmas, but he got sent to Italy."

Anna, Lydi and Michael listened as the woman poured out the story of her grandson. He lost both parents in a tragic accident when he was only seven. Sena had raised him as her own. The day he turned 17, he joined the Marines, realizing his dream, and has been serving his country ever since. Furloughs with his grandmother were the only times she got to see him. They both faithfully wrote letters, but Levi had warned his grandmother that during the war he may not be able to write often, and he could not reveal his location or activities, in case the mail should fall into enemy hands.

As Sena spoke, her eyes focused on a single shelf attached to the wall before her. On the shelf was a model wooden ship and a small picture frame. In the frame was a newspaper clipping with a photograph of a very young man in uniform. All at once she looked at Michael. "Boy, I do hope the war will be done before you get old enough to fight."

Anna frowned for a moment, as though such a thought had never occurred to her. After a few seconds she stood. "Thank you for inviting us in, Mrs. Gullickson. You should be very proud of your grandson, and we pray that he will be safe." Glancing to Lydi, she added, "We brought some of our Christmas baking to share with you."

The young girl held out a package and forced a smile in spite of the fear that had just crept into her heart. She gave the old woman a polite nod, but the lump in her throat would not allow her to speak. A nagging dread engulfed Lydi as she stared at the clipping, considering the old woman's words. Surely the dreadful battles could not rage for years! The idea of Michael growing up during the war and having to fight made her want to scream. Suddenly, she thought of Benjamin.

CHAPTER 9

A MOTHER

Someone was knocking at the door. Didn't they know she did not want to see anyone? Since two of her boys were gone, the mother barely managed to get out of bed each morning, but her Scandinavian heritage demanded that she invite guests in and offer them coffee, at least. As she shuffled through the entry, she wondered if there were any sweets in the pantry to serve them. Ida had baked her special Date Pinwheel Cookies. There should be some left. Mabel had made spice cake with cooked brown sugar frosting, but that was yesterday. There was nothing fresh. Was it just last week she had baked every day for her boys?

Selma Svenson opened the entry door and greeted her visitors. "Oh, hello, Mrs. Andersson. And the children. Please come in." She led them into the kitchen and invited them to sit. "I will put on the coffee pot."

"No, thank you, we cannot stay." Anna sat on the edge of her chair. "We brought you some cookies." Lydi set the package on the table and smiled up at her friends' mother, whose brows were etched with worry lines.

"Ah, thank you, Lydi." Selma patted Lydi's arm. "My girls, they always speak of you. You are good friend for them." Her gaze turned to Michael. "And they talk of Michael and his smart sheep." Michael grinned proudly, though he was chafing to get outside. He had enough visiting for one day. The sad look returned to the woman's eyes. "Your sheep and your ma, they are lucky you are too young to fight in the war."

"We hope your boys will return home safely," Anna said quietly. "If there is anything our family can do to help, you just have your girls tell Lydi."

"That is very kind, but we will be good."

Chore-time drew near. The Andersson's headed home after saying thanks and goodbyes. Selma sat again at her kitchen table and stared at the gift Lydi had brought. At last she carried it to the pantry and said to herself, "Maybe I will make something good for supper."

Twenty minutes later, Adolf stomped the snow off his overshoes and strode into the kitchen. He studied his wife for a few moments as she added chunks of wood to the cook stove, then replaced the burner and set a kettle on top of it. He laid a brown paper package on the table and finally spoke. "Chet at the store sent this home for you. He said a woman in Canterbury is sewing these for all the families of servicemen."

She gave her husband a questioning look before untying the string. Folded inside was a small quilt-like piece of fabric. There was a white backing. On the front a red strip was sewn all the way around to form a frame. In the center, on white, were two blue stars. The woman ran her fingers over the stars.

"It is called a service flag," Adolf said, "or a Mother's Flag," he added softly. "One star is for Elmer. One is for Arthur. It is supposed to hang in the window."

Selma shook her head in silence.

"We are supposed to be proud that we have sons fighting for our country," the man spoke in a tone of reproach; he had grown weary of his wife's continued despair since two sons had gone.

She drew in a deep breath and straightened her spine. Her eyes flashed as she replied to her husband. "I will be proud when they are home safe." Then she carefully folded the flag and carried it to the living room. She gently paced it on the lamp table next to the Bible. Adolf did not see her bow her head and squeeze her eyes shut as she tenderly covered the two blue stars with her hands.

CHAPTER 10

LETTER FROM BILLIE

Ethel handed an envelope to Lydi as she walked into the morning classroom. Lydi's eyes shone as she read the return address: Oak Creek, Colorado. "A letter from Billie!" Her friend and teacher nodded with a smug smile. Lydi could hardly wait until the noon recess to read it.

January 12, 1942

Dear Ethel, Lydi, Mabel, Julia and Lilly,

I am so happy that our family moved to Oak Creek! Pa and Ma are happier, too. Pa's new boss at the mine says President Roosevelt wants more coal for manufacturing war planes. There is a shortage of workers since the young men have en-listed, so the miners are getting paid more. For the first time I can remember, there is money left after all the bills are paid.

Most of the miners at Twenty Mile Mine live in our little coal town. The Mori family, who immi-grated to our country from Japan three years ago, live right across the street. He works with Pa at the mine. Because Mr. Mori is smaller than the other men, he can fit into narrow tunnels down in the mine and move very quickly. He has saved his crew twice from falling rock for which we are all very grateful.

Mr. and Mrs. Mori have a son and two daugh-ters. The youngest daughter is Akito, and she has become my very best friend! Since our school teacher went back to California over Christmas va-cation, we had two whole weeks off! Every day we spent at either her house or mine, or exploring the woods behind the town.

Akito and I made up a secret code. It is so fun to write in cipher that no one else can understand. My sister Dru and Akito's sister, Yuna, have been trying to crack it. That will never happen!

On days that we spend at her house we make up little skits that we present for our mothers. Akito is a great actress and singer. She sings a song in Japanese about a young man who must leave his girlfriend and go to war. I do not understand all the words yet, but even the melody makes me feel sad.

When I visit the Mori's home I need to remember my manners, or rather remember the Japanese customs. Everyone takes off their shoes just inside the door and puts on slippers. Once I went running inside to find Akito and forgot to take off my shoes. Her mother was not happy with me. Then there are the chopsticks! The first night I was asked to stay for supper I tried to learn how to use them. Picking up grains of rice with two skinny sticks is just about impossible in my book! Then we were talking about

59

one of our plays and I got so excited I was pointing and swinging the chopsticks. Akito and Yuna were staring at me as if I had just swallowed a toad. Later, they informed me that such use of chopsticks was extremely rude. The worst part, though, was when I could not get the piece of chicken to stay on the chopsticks, so I just jabbed that meat with one of the chopsticks. I heard a gasp from Akito and saw the look of shock on her face. Quickly I stuffed the chicken in my mouth and chewed away. When I dared to peek up at Mr. Mori I am pretty sure he was trying to hide a grin!

One week after Christmas, Akito's brother, Shin, announced that he was joining the army. After what happened at Pearl Harbor I thought it would be very difficult for him to fight. "What if you have to shoot at those Japanese soldiers?" I asked him. "They might be your relatives!"

He lifted his chin and declared, "I am American. I fight for America!"

Shin's parents were very proud. They had a special celebration in honor of their son's going off to war. There are things about the Japanese culture I just don't understand. Why would you be happy that your son is going to war?

How are things in Iowa? Are there a lot of young men from Canterbury enlisting?

Pa says the war will change everything. I am just glad we aren't poor anymore. And, I have the best friend a girl could ask for. I can't wait for summer when Akito and I can be together every day! I am so glad I don't have to worry about some outlandish war.

I had to write you about how happy I am here.

Love and miss you all.

Billie

CHAPTER 11

PROJECT REACH

Miss Bollinger had announced at school on Wednesday that there would be a meeting on Friday for anyone who wished to volunteer to help support the war effort on the Homefront. Lydi had heard the younger children discuss it at recess. At 3:45 on Friday, February 6, the teacher reminded her students of their weekend assignments, then stated that it was time for a "REACH" meeting, and that anyone who did not wish to participate in the group may be dismissed early.

Every child remained in their seat.

Overwhelmed and a bit nervous, Lydi stood to address her fellow students at Chaucer Township School Number Seven. She explained how the idea for such a group had come about in a conversation about Homefront support and how it could help win the war. Her gaze swept over the classroom of more than twenty youngsters, ranging in age from five to seventeen. "Can you think of things we can do to help?" No one spoke. The tension in the room was palpable.

Finally, Emma, Lilly and Mabel's younger sister, slowly raised her hand. "I heard that there are soldiers in hospitals who don't have anybody at home. Do you think we could write them letters?"

"Emma, that is a great idea!" Lydi smiled. Children nodded. Feet shuffled. Other hands raised.

"I think my dad has addresses of military hospitals," offered Benjamin Hindricks, whose father owned the town drugstore. "We know all the soldiers from around Canterbury. They might like to get letters from us, too." Lydi wondered if she blushed as his eyes met hers when he spoke.

Benjamin's younger brother, Adam, joined in. "We could shovel sidewalks for their families when it snows again."

Lydi's eyes shone brightly at every suggestion, and she brought forth one of her own. "I can't help but think that the men on the battlefields must wear holes in their socks. Does anyone know how to knit?"

Lilly and Julia's hands went up simultaneously and the other girls giggled. "We learned to knit when we were five," Lilly spoke shyly, then glanced at her twin sister, who nodded with a smile. "We'd be willing to teach people how to knit, but we will need yarn and knitting needles." Mabel grinned at her sisters while she took notes for the group.

Miss Bollinger stood then. Tears threatened as she looked out over her classroom. She had never dreamed that a teacher could feel so much love, so much pride for her students. "You have shared excellent ideas today. Keep thinking over the weekend. We can meet again next week to plan how to put your thoughts into action."

Most of the students filed out to the entry to don their winter coats and mittens. Lydi, Mabel, Julia and Lilly remained. Miss Bollinger, the teacher, became Ethel, the dear friend. Only these five, the founders of REACH, knew what the letters stood for. They had decided to keep it secret in case the German army ever did manage to invade America. The group might be able to continue its work under the cover of REACH, an innocent group of volunteer students helping out in their community. For now, at least, it was best that the others did not know the words that formed the acronym: Ready for Every Action to Crush Hitler.

Little Vicky and Ricky Christleton remained in their desks. They had sat quietly throughout the meeting while Vicky thoughtfully contemplated every proposal. Noticing the distressed frown darkening the child's face, Lydi moved to her side and crouched down to eye level. "Vicky, do you have a question?"

The five-year-old glanced over at her twin brother and heaved a great sigh. "Everybody just seems so worried. So sad. What can we do to make them happy again?"

CHAPTER 12

DUTY, HONOR, FAMILY

"No, Paul, you can't do this. Please tell me you won't." Becky Evans implored her husband, as her shoulders slumped. Her chest hurt and she could barely breathe. She felt as if the wind had been knocked out of her.

He wrapped his arms around her, resting his chin on her head. "Ah, Becky, the army needs doctors desperately. Already, injured soldiers are filling the military hospitals."

She breathed in the scent of this man she loved. His heart beat in a slow, solid rhythm as her own pounded wildly in her throat. "Let the younger doctors go, the ones who do not have wives…or babies." She thought of little Mary Ann, already asleep for the night, snug in her crib.

"Those men have mothers and fathers who love them. Little sisters. Grandmas. Someone will miss them just as much." He pulled her closer as her body swayed to the side, not realizing that he was holding her up. The man felt cruel for putting her through this, but he had no choice. "What would people think if I stayed here in safety and comfort while all the others are going off to war? It is my duty, Becky." She sniffed, then shook her head slightly, still nestled against his warm chest.

"Gus will help out here in my office until I come home. He tried to enlist, but failed the physical. They said he has a heart murmur. You and Lydi can help him run the surgery. If you want, I can even train you in midwifery."

A small puff of air escaped her lungs and she turned her head up to see her husband's eyes. "I do not wish to bring babies into the world. Not this cruel, war-filled place. I want our baby to have her father at home." She placed her hands over his heart. "Paul, you know how I get. I cannot handle this, having you leave us, having you go to war."

"You mean your melancholy moods? Those feelings of desolation often occur after women have babies. It is simply their bodies changing rapidly, and, of course the responsibility of a new life. You are better now. Nothing to worry about." He placed his hands on her shoulders and looked into his wife's tear-filled eyes. "I will come home, Becky, I promise."

She wanted to pound his chest, beg him to stay home, but she let her hands fall to her sides in resignation and trudged slowly to the bedroom. She bent to kiss baby Mary Ann's downy head and listened for a second to her soft breathing. Then she quietly stepped out of her shoes and, not bothering to change into her nightgown, crawled into bed.

CHAPTER 13

SCHOOL BOY BILL

Ethel Bollinger rode a horse to school every day. She did not consider this anything unusual or extraordinary. It was a matter of necessity, actually. Her mother and sister had jobs in town and needed the car. Besides, she loved her horse.

She recalled when they had read the ad in the *Canterbury Times-News* and driven almost to Sioux City to see the retired race horse last summer. Bill had long, strong legs and stood very tall, "nearly 18 hands," the old rancher bragged to Ethel and her mother, "trained to neck reign. He's got five gaits: walk, trot, canter, gallop and back." He rubbed the horse's muzzle, affectionately. "But, he's done racin,' this big ol' boy."

He spat in the clean straw in the next stall and studied the young girl for a few seconds. "You're gonna be up there pretty high, ridin' this horse, but ya still need something to sit on." He hobbled over to the tack room and came out with a well-worn saddle. "I'll throw in this for five bucks," he said as he plopped it over the wooden fence post. "Good horse. Good saddle. Good deal."

Ethel had bought School Boy Bill and his saddle for $55. Her mother had to sign the bank loan for her, even though Ethel was eighteen and earning the money herself, teaching at her one-room school. Bill quickly became the young girl's friend and companion, greeting her each day with a soft nicker as she rubbed his smooth head.

Today he waited patiently while the girl gently placed a soft woolen blanket on his back, one Mother had made, then stood on the fence rail to get the saddle on his back. "Good Boy," she murmured.

He rubbed his head against her shoulder and she climbed up into the saddle.

On the rides to school, Bill seemed to understand that his rider would have a long ways to fall. He never bucked or spooked. On frigid winter mornings, the neighbor closest to the school led the animal to his barn and tossed him a flake of hay, then brought him back, to be waiting for the young teacher when her work day was over. On warm spring days, Ethel tied her beloved horse to the hitching post north of the building and he nibbled fresh shoots of green grass and dandelions that emerged from the newly-warmed earth. At recess the students fed the teacher's horse their apple cores, which he gently lifted from their hands with his soft lips, his big brown eyes shining with thanks.

On this warm sunny day in April, School Boy Bill stood contentedly, his ears flickering toward the open windows, taking in the voices of his mistress and her students.

Inside, Miss Bollinger smiled proudly at the stacks of knitted socks, bars of soap and handkerchiefs that were arranged neatly on the front of her desk. Each morning students brought items to be sent overseas to the soldiers, part of their Project REACH. Once a week Anna Andersson stopped to take the items to Bellum's store, where they were packed and sent to the Red Cross Office in Council Bluffs. Today the stack was so tall it threatened to block her view of the students.

Reading followed history. Most of the class were reading silently from the books they had chosen from the small set of shelves that made up the school library. A few of the younger group were reading out loud. The teacher moved to sit in a desk next to Ricky as he sounded out the words in his first-grade primer while his twin sister followed along. Suddenly a sound carried through the open window, a snort from School Boy Bill, as he blew air out his nostrils. Teacher and students' heads lifted, listened. Hearing no further sound, they went on with their studies. A few minutes later, a much louder sound, an anxious whinny shrilled, this time from the opposite side of the school followed by the pounding of galloping hoofs. The woman's eyes flew to Michael who jumped up and raced outside while the others flocked to the window. The boy soon came into view leading Bill by his reigns. The horse tossed his head and danced to the right as his head turned back to where Michael had found him. He whinnied again and pawed at the ground. Michael ran his hand down the animal's side, speaking in soothing tones until at last the horse calmed and began to crop blades of green grass.

All heads turned as Michael returned to the class and apprised his teacher. "Somebody tried to steal Bill, Miss Bollinger. He must have bucked them off when they got to the top of the hill. I heard voices, then saw a couple guys heading into the woods. One of them was limping pretty bad." The teacher frowned, but thanked Michael as he strode to his desk, breathless with excitement. As he dropped into his seat he added with a grin, "Bill was headed back to the school. Smart Boy."

Several times that afternoon, Ethel found herself gravitating to the open window. She peered outside to check on her horse. School Boy Bill must have been watching for her, too. His ears tipped, he stretched his nose high in the air, nostrils quivering, searching. Then he nodded his great head and nickered softly. Ethel loved that horse.

CHAPTER 14

TWO FOOTED WEASELS

"Supper was most delectable, as always," Geoffrey thanked his sister-in-law as he stood to carry his plate to the sink. He then filled both cast iron kettles with fresh water from the pump and placed them on the back of the stove. There would be hot water for washing in the morning.

William and Christina finished their tea, then began their usual after-supper routine. She washed the dishes. William dried. Geoffrey added chunks of wood to the stoves and escaped to the living room where he turned the knobs on the Zenith, got it "warmed up," he called it. The three had come to enjoy nights sitting in their rocking chairs in front of the radio. He tuned in the station for *The Jack*

Benny Program. They would laugh out loud at the antics of Jack and the other actors. Laughter was a good thing, Geoffrey often reminded himself, especially in these uncertain times.

Suddenly Romeo and Juliet poked their heads into the living room. Their beds were in the entry and the well-trained dogs never crossed into the living room. Romeo gave a slight bark and then whined as he stared imploringly at Geoffrey. "What is it, Boy? What is bothering you?" Geoffrey shuffled to the loyal border collies. Romeo turned his body to face the outside door, sniffed the air and emitted a low growl. Geoffrey reached for the door handle after giving the dogs the "stay" command. A mountain lion had been sighted near Underwood, and he would not risk losing the animals' lives to a lion. He stepped out on the front porch and surveyed the farm. A full moon illuminated the night and the stars seemed close enough to touch. A gentle breeze rustled through the bright new leaves on the cottonwood. The sheep in the north pasture rested peacefully. The lambs nestled next to their mothers, who bleated soft comforts. Prince stood majestically behind the fence across the road, his herd of Jersey cattle lolling through the soft meadow. A blade of grass flashed in the moonlight as it fell from the bull's mouth, twirling to the ground.

Geoffrey peered out toward the barn and chicken coop in the front, seeing nothing amiss. The doors were all secured for the night. No animal could get in the buildings. Satisfied that all was well, the old farmer went back inside. He petted his dogs' heads affectionately. "Does the full moon have you riled, Romey? Nothing out there to worry about." He made a motion with his hand and each collie turned around three times and curled onto its blanket, though Romeo grumbled a small protest.

Don Wilson was announcing *The Jack Benny Program* on the Zenith as Geoffrey returned to his chair. Christina's knitting needles were flashing out the cuffs of a brown sock. The three settled in for a relaxing evening of listening. "...with our own Jack Benny, Mary Livingstone and Rochester." Music poured out of the wireless as the ads began.

Romeo growled and gave a sharp bark and again pushed his head into the living room. He snorted and shook his furry mane, then whimpered as his big brown eyes sought Geoffrey's. With a sigh, the man heaved himself up. He reached for the shotgun that hung over the door, the trusty Winchester 97 Pump. Michael's report of someone trying to steal School Boy Bill at school that day flashed through his head. Again, he gave the dogs the command to stay and headed outside.

The wind that came from the direction of the barn washed over him, but this time it was tainted. Was that smoke? Alarmed, the man scanned the buildings for dreaded black tendrils or ominous clouds that meant fire. He could see nothing. The odor persisted until he realized it was the smell of food, something roasting. Shotgun under his arm, he circled slowly around the chicken coop and barn, thinking he would slink up close to whatever, whomever was causing the smoke, without being detected. At the corner of the barn he heard voices. He stopped. Listened.

"Aw, Earl, you worry too much!" There was a sizzling sound, like something dripping on a fire. "You gotta be more like me. I pour my worries out." A different voice uttered a mocking groan, but no words. "We won't never get caught, Earl. Heck. Nobody knows where we are. The draft board in Kansas can't get their paws on us if they can't find us. We won't never have to go to war. We can just keep goin' from farm to farm, eatin' like kings." The last words were muffled, obviously mingled with chewing.

Geoffrey heard a rustle of movement, then a grunt and an ungentlemanly curse as though someone had just plopped to the ground.

"How's your leg, Earl? If you'd a seen yerself fallin' off that horse, you'd be laughin,' too. You flew like a bird, you did." A bout of sniggers and snorts went on until, "OWW, why'd you throw that rock at me? That hurt."

"Buford, you TALK too much!" Earl had obviously had enough.

Having heard all he needed to know, Geoffrey waited, willing himself to be patient though he was seething inside at these lily-livered weasels who called themselves men. After a few minutes of silence, he eased around the corner. "Good evening, gentlemen," he bluffed in a friendly voice. "Something certainly smells enticing out here." The intruders sat up with a start, saw the gun and gradually settled back to eating. One knelt close to the fire, grease running down his whiskers. The other sat opposite, his leg sprawled in front of him, hand resting on it as if to will away the pain.

"Howdy!" The talker smiled weakly, glancing quickly at his partner, then back up to Geoffrey. "Hey, help yerself to some chicken." He moved to hand him a stick with a charred drumstick on the end. Earl glared at him. "Uh, we BOUGHT the chicken at a STORE." He smiled smugly at Earl, who just shook his head and stared into the fire. "You gotta 'scuze Earl, here. He's hurtin.' He took a fall today, a really BIG fall." The man flung his head back and cackled with laughter. "Earl fell off a big h... OWW, another rock, Earl? Oh, yeah." Another chortle burst out as Buford chattered on, careful to avoid Earl's glare. "Earl fell off a big HOUSE."

Geoffrey braced his feet then, thinking his mother would not approve of his thoughts at the moment. He pumped a shell into the chamber of the 97 and lifted the barrel. He had their attention.

Reaching into his left pocket, he managed to find his wallet. He threw a wad of bills on the ground next to the injured man. "The train stops in Canterbury in the morning. You get on that train and go back to Kansas, and you deal with the draft like men. While you are traveling, you think about our boys, some barely 16 years old, fighting over in Europe. They enlisted. They wanted to serve their country. They are dying so Hitler won't come here and get the likes of you."

Earl stared into the flames, not moving a muscle. Buford dropped his chicken into the fire. Geoffrey continued. "Just in the event that you might consider stealing any more chickens---or horses..." The gentleman stifled a spiteful grin, imagining School Boy Bill sending Earl skyward. "By tomorrow every farmer in the area and every sheriff in the state will be on the lookout for two draft evaders."

Buford began to splutter. Earl yelled, "Shut up!"

With a twinkle in his eye, Geoffrey lifted the gun to point skyward. "Of course, you chaps know everyone who goes to jail now gets sent to Germany. Yes, sir. They get hauled to the front lines. You do know what happens there, right?" Buford's mouth hung open. His eyes were round as they watched the farmer walk away.

Back inside, Don Wilson was crooning the ending credits for Jack Benny's show. Music poured out of the radio. Christina looked up in concern. Geoffrey waited in his rocker. His eyes met his brother's. After a few seconds of silent communication, William nodded with a grin, then said sincerely, "You missed the show. I am sorry, Brother."

Geoffrey stretched his arms and yawned a great yawn, excusing his lack of manners to Christina. "Do not worry about me, William. I enjoyed

84

my own show, complete with picture as well as sound." He shook his head, chuckled to himself and rubbed his hands together. "I do believe mine was even more amusing than Jack Benny's."

CHAPTER 15

BILLIE'S NOTE

March 30, 1942

Dear Ethel, Lydi, Mabel, Lilly and Julia,

The most dreadful thing has happened! My best friend and all her family are gone. Soldiers came and loaded them into trucks and took them away. I am so mad I could spit!

Akito and Yuni and their mom and dad came over last night to tell us they would be leaving. Mr. Miso explained that after the bombing of Pearl Harbor, President Roosevelt signed a law that ordered all people of Japanese descent to be taken to concentration camps. He said that some people in the government do not trust anyone of Japanese ancestry, even the ones born in America. They think that these people might be spies or traitors to our country. That is so ridiculous! Shin Miso just joined the army to fight the war for America!

Their family was given 24 hours' notice and informed that each person could bring one bag. Akito brought me all her special things that she could not take. She said I could have them, but I have tucked that bag under my bed and when she gets back, I will give them back to her.

Right now I am not very proud of my country, and I just want this stupid war to be over!

I will write if I find out anything else. I hope things are not so sad in Iowa.

Love,

Billie

Upset and angry that Billie's friends had been treated so harshly, Ethel, Lydi, Mabel, Julia and

Lilly stared at each other in disbelief. They left school that day in silence, each lost in her own thoughts.

CHAPTER 16

SACRIFICE

"Use it up – Wear it out – Make it do - or Do Without!" Geoffrey perused the newest war posters tacked to the bulletin board at Bellum's Mercantile. One placard in particular caught his eye. "Scrap Metal Needed! Help build tanks for our soldiers!"

Chet Bellum glanced up from his receipt book at the front counter. He was aware of Geoffrey's attempt to join the air force and how devastated the older farmer was when he was rejected. "You lookin' to help win the war?" Chet caught himself before adding, "even if you can't be a soldier."

Geoffrey's head was bent as he looked over his round wire-rimmed spectacles to read the smaller print. "18 tons of scrap metal go into one tank," He read out loud, then whistled softly at the thought.

"Louise and I painted an old barrel and set it out front for collecting stuff. People bring in tin cans. Kids throw in gum wrappers. Guess aluminum is in high demand. Even cigarette packages have a foil lining that can be salvaged," Chet added with a satisfied nod. "Every little bit helps." The man sighed and turned back to his notebook. "18 tons is a lot of gum wrappers."

Resolutely, Geoffrey turned suddenly to face his friend. "Chet, would you be willing to inform your customers that I can transport large metal items for them? Most certainly there are plow shares and old cream cans lying about. William and I will drive them to the government drop-off center in Council Bluffs."

"I sure will tell people," Chet promised, as he set his fountain pen on the counter. "Better yet, how about if you make your own poster to put up?" He ripped a sheet of paper from the back of his note-book, then watched while the gentleman farmer penned the words, in perfect script. Then he sketched a battle tank with a gun on the front and signed his name with a flourish. With a hint of a smile, Geoffrey strode back to the bulletin board. He found a shiny metal thumbtack up in the corner. He stared at it a few seconds thinking it could be used to build a tank, then thoughtfully pushed it into the cork to fasten his notice.

That night Geoffrey, William and Christina laughed out loud at the shenanigans of *Fibber McGee and Molly* as the episode played on the Zen-ith. Harlow Wilcox's voice resounded from the box. "Help win the war! Every American needs to get in the scrap. Tin cans, bits of copper and steel, toys, pots and pans. Bring it to your local collection center…"

William stood to turn off the radio. "There it is, my brother, another way we can help with the war effort at home. Every gram of metal collected will facilitate construction of war machinery." His gaze met his brother's. "Of course, the war will require sacrifice by all of us."

The man turned to the stairs and did not see Geoffrey's smirk as he looked down, rubbed his hands together and whispered, "Indubitably."

Early the next morning Christina smelled fresh coffee as she slipped her gingham apron over her head and tied the strings in the back. In the kitchen Geoffrey was sitting at the table. He wolfed down a spoon of oatmeal as he nodded a greeting to his sister-in-law. The ceiling creaked above them, an indication that William was also up and about. With a quick upward glance, Geoffrey pushed back his chair and placed his bowl in the sink. "There is a pot of oatmeal on the back of the stove," he said. The thud, thud of stocking feet pounding down stair steps echoed from the living room. "Ah, well, I am off to the barn. Chores await!" Geoffrey grabbed his coat and boots and hastily rushed out the back door.

William stormed into the kitchen a few seconds later. "Where is that brother of mine?" he bellowed. Then he strode to the door and flung it open, but Geoffrey was already out of sight. Grumbling, he shut the door and turned back to his wife. "How, my dear Christina, am I to do chores wearing this?"

He reached for the suspenders that hung down the back of his bib overalls, grabbed one by the end and pulled it over his shoulder. The stitching on the blue and gray striped fabric had been ripped open and the metal fastener was gone. Christina noticed that a small hole remained where a metal button had once been. The buckle and button had served to connect the straps to the bib of the overalls. She looked away from William as she struggled to hide her grin.

Meanwhile, in the barn, Geoffrey settled onto his stool, leaning his head into dear old Bessy's hip joint and began to milk her. The sound of the liquid squirting into the steel bucket muffled the farmer's chuckle as he imagined William seething over his missing suspender clasps. "Of course, my dear brother, the war will require sacrifice by all of us."

Bessy turned her head to stare in wonder at her farmer.

CHAPTER 17

LAST DAY OF SCHOOL

A soft breeze drifted in through the school-house windows as Miss Bollinger prepared her students for dismissal. The walls were bare. Drawings and reports had been taken down and stacked on desks, all to be carried home at the end of the day, carefully tucked between books and report cards. *"Have a good summer!"* and *"Continue Project REACH if the War Continues"* were chalked in neat cursive on the blackboard.

The group had planned their summer REACH actions. Since they would have little contact with each other over the summer, Lydi had asked Chet Bellum if he would allow a notebook on his counter at the mercantile that would be accessible to the students. All were encouraged to read and add comments to the book each time they came to town, indicating what services they had performed as well as what needed to be done to help the families most affected by the war. For many of the youngsters, this would be their only communication with the others during the summer months.

As chairman of Operation REACH, Lydi thanked the class for the knitted socks and scarves that the teacher had already packed into boxes for the soldiers. Two of the younger boys had promised to bring their wagon to town and collect scrap metal for the collection barrel at the mercantile.

"We can keep writing letters," Lydi reminded everyone with a glance at the Christleton twins, who were focused on coloring and writing something at their desks.

Mabel raised her hand, and after a warm nod from the teacher, she added, "Our brothers love getting letters. They get lonely over in Germany, and I guess it helps to know someone back here cares." Her sister, Emma, nodded in agreement, but Chaucer Township School Number Seven remained ominously still.

The young teacher stepped forward. Her students were already heartsick, worried about the outcome of the war. People discussed it during the day. Newscasts blared it over the wires every evening. She did not know how her announcement would affect her class, but it needed to be made. Her first student would be going off to war. With what she hoped was a calm, encouraging smile, Miss Bollinger shared, "We will add Lem's name to our letter writing list. Lem has joined the army and will be leaving next week." Her eyes turned to the young man sitting alone in the back row. "We wish you the best, Lem." A lump formed in Lem's throat. He tried to swallow. He tried to speak, but managed only a curt nod before turning his eyes down to his desk.

Suddenly the breeze deserted them, stealing the oxygen from the room. Lydi's gaze quickly skirted to Benjamin. He felt it and their eyes met for a moment. Then Lydi looked up at the words on the blackboard. "*...if the war continues.*" Lem had just turned 17. There would be other birthdays. More boys would soon come of age.

Ethel Bollinger contemplated the students in her one-room school. It was the last day of the year. The children should have been ready to burst with excitement to begin their summer vacation. Instead, frowns of doubt clouded their faces.

The stack of papers was growing taller on Ricky's desk. The two seemed oblivious to the oppressive mood hovering in the room. Vicky stopped coloring as her twin counted softly. "Forty-seven, forty-eight, forty-nine, FIFTY!" Vicky cheerfully tamped the papers together in a neat pile.

The twins both smiled as Vicky held the papers up and addressed the teacher. There was a big red heart colored in the center. At the top of each one Vicky had written, "Dear Mr. Soldier, we love you." At the bottom her brother had added, "Ricky and Vicky."

Vicky beamed at her brother as they carried the letters to the teacher's desk. Vicky breathed a satisfied sigh. "Just doing something makes me feel happier inside."

A whisper of fresh air trickled back into the school.

CHAPTER 18

UNUSUAL PRESCRIPTION

It was Dr. Gustavson's first day of office hours at the surgery in Canterbury. The first day since Dr. Evans had left on the soldier train. Becky Evans sat dolefully at the front desk with baby Mary Ann on her lap. Lydi welcomed and seated visitors, then found their file, if there was one, in Dr. Evans' drawer, and took it to the new doctor. She ushered the patient to the examining room, then returned to the waiting room to help out in any way possible.

Just before noon, Selma Svenson shuffled in slowly, her husband Adolf's arm wrapped around her elbow. Lydi welcomed the couple and invited them to sit until the doctor was ready. Dr. Gus soon entered. He introduced himself and shook hands with them. Adolf spoke for his wife. "Selma's been having troubles. I brought her in to see you." The doctor nodded a smile and then escorted the woman to the exam room, taking note of her slow progress.

"I get awful cramps in my legs all the time. I don't know what's wrong, Doctor." She watched warily as he helped her onto the examination table and pulled a chair directly in front of her.

"Well, let's figure out what the problem is, Mrs. Svenson." He checked both her ears, then looked into her eyes. "Your eyes are red, bloodshot. Have you had that very long?"

"Ja, about the same time the leg pains started, my eyes got red, and my heart started pounding in my chest. Every day this happens."

He listened to her heart with his stethoscope for several minutes. The patient began to worry that something was amiss. Finally, with stethoscope still in place, he asked, "Did all these symptoms, these changes in your body, happen at once?"

"They all happened back in December."

"Was there anything else going on? Something that caused stress? Worry?"

"Ja, my boys, two of them went off to the war."

With a deep sigh, the doctor pushed his chair back and looked into his patient's eyes. "Do you cry a lot, worrying about your boys?"

"I did. Not anymore. Now, I just pray."

He nodded and smiled gently. "Mrs. Svenson, I cannot find anything terribly wrong. Your heart sounds strong. When you are upset, sometimes your body rebels. I think you might be dehydrated. Do you drink much water?"

She stared at him, aghast. "I am a Swede, and Swedes drink coffee, not water."

The doctor stood then and touched her shoulder. "I think the muscle spasms will go away if you drink water, too. Try to drink two big glasses of water, one right away in the morning." Then he chuckled, "Plus your coffee. And, it would not hurt if you drink extra milk and eat vegetables. Do you have a garden?"

Her mouth dropped open and she flashed him another incredulous stare. "Of course we have a garden. We grow everything we need to eat, except sugar. And coffee."

Mrs. Svenson, I have a feeling you will be fine in a week or so. You just work on doing those things I suggested." Dr. Gustavson guided her to the waiting room.

Adolf stood then, went to the desk and paid for the appointment. When he and Selma were outside, he looked at her questioningly. "Well, what did the doctor say?"

She stopped short of the car door and turned to her husband, shaking her head in obvious doubt. "What did I tell you, Adolf? I wonder what kind of doctor this man is. He prescribed a glass of water!"

CHAPTER 19

THE INTERNMENT CAMP

"You just leave that letter from your friend on the REACH notebook, Miss Bollinger. I think nearly everybody from school stops in to see what's in it." Chet Bellum thought the booklet on his corner counter was a good means of communication. It did not hurt his business at the mercantile, either.

Ethel thanked the proprietor of Bellum's Store and left Billie's latest letter. She was thankful that this letter was more hopeful than the last as she remembered her cousin's news.

May 20, 1942
Dear Ethel and all,

In my last letter I was dreadfully upset because my best friend and her family had been forced to leave their home. The government had ordered that people of Japanese ancestry be taken to Internment Camps. This happened because Japan bombed Pearl Harbor and Americans are angry and therefore suspicious of Japanese immigrants.

I finally got a letter from Akito. She lives only sixty miles from here! The place is called Amache and is near Granada, Colorado. The place is still being built, and the Mori family are helping. Can you imagine constructing your own prison?

Akito said it is not so bad. They live in a building that has six family units. Each unit, or large room has an open closet, a coal stove and two folding cots with mattresses. There are loose bricks on the dirt floor. Six of these units share a large shower and bathroom area and a mess hall where everyone goes to eat meals.

There are eight machine gun posts around the camp which is surrounded by a barbed wire fence. Akito and her sister, Yuna, were frightened at first, but they have made friends with the guards, who are Army Privates. One young guard brought a football to the camp and every day he teaches the young boys how to play football and they play catch for hours.

Once the housing is finished, a school and hospital will be built. Mr. Mori is a spokesperson for the prisoners. He says the government men in charge of the camp are reasonable and open to ideas from the Japanese. Plans are in the works for growing vegetables and having shops where the people can work.

Some of the internees cook the meals at the mess hall. They have to cook with what is provided, and there are few ingredients available that are used in Japanese cooking. No rice, only potatoes and noodles. Some of the residents refuse to eat the food, but Mr. Mori tells them they must eat to remain strong.

I am proud of Akito and her family. She says they must make the best of things until the war is over. How long can it go on? I know I say this every letter, but I do so hate war.

How are things in Iowa? The REACH project sounds impressive. I am so proud of you and your friends for doing something to make a difference on the home front.

I will keep you posted on Akito as well as what goes on here at the coal camp. I enjoy getting your letters.

Love,

Your Cousin and Friend, Billie

CHAPTER 20

MEASURING UP

"Quick! Read Sena's chart! She's on her way and will be out to test the new doctor." Lydi hurried to the file, procured a folder and handed it to Dr. Gustavson. His eyes rolled to the ceiling and he shook his head with a grin before focusing on the notes his predecessor had written. Becky sat quietly in the rocking chair in the corner of the waiting room. Baby Mary Ann was snuggled into her mother's neck, sound asleep.

Suddenly a quick, solid knock sounded at the door, and it creaked open. The cane entered first, a twisted, hand-carved specimen that gleamed in the light. Only the bottom tip was scratched and worn and it made a hollow sound as it tapped on the wooden floor of the clinic. Soon a wrinkled hand, splotched with age spots, came into view, wrapped around the crook of the cane. At last the top of her head slowly appeared, bent over the cane. Thin wisps of white hair escaped the bounds of a braid that was twisted in a tight circle on the top of her head. Like a tiny shield, it inched closer to the desk with each tap of the cane.

"Good morning, Sena!" Lydi called from behind the counter, sending Dr. Gus an encouraging smile as he slipped the chart back onto the desk.

The braid-shield lifted slightly as the woman peered over her glasses. "Where is that new young doctor? I heard he's not worth a hill of beans!" She stopped with a final clunk of her cane.

Dr. Gustavson stepped forward, reaching out his hand. "This must be the lovely young woman Dr. Evans spoke of so fondly."

"Humph! You're either blinder than me or you are just plan full of it, lad." With a small sniff, her gaze turned to the ceiling, but her eyelashes fluttered. She added softly, "The good doctor spoke of me, did he?"

"He said you have an extremely kind heart and that you make the best tomato preserves on the planet."

She slipped her left hand into her patched apron pocket, produced a small jar, and placed it in the doctor's hand. "My last jar. I just planted my tomato plants so I will make more this fall."

"Thank you, Sena. I will enjoy this on my toast in the morning. Now, how about if I take a quick listen to that heart?"

"Well, I don't have money for an appointment. Don't need one."

"Oh, no appointment is necessary. I can just listen right here." She stood quietly while he held the stethoscope on her back, then looked up at him questioningly.

"Your heart sounds fine, Sena."

"Good. I want to be around when my grandson comes home. He is in Italy now, fighting for his country. Just got promoted, he did. To Sergeant First Class." A wistful smile crossed her face. Then she remembered her purpose for the visit. "Doctor, I don't need an appointment, but do you think you could just quick look at my eyes? I don't see so good anymore. Maybe there's something you can do for them."

"Of course, Sena, I will do that. Can you just turn your head up toward the light?" Her face lifted slightly toward the window as the man gently lifted her chin and stared into her pale blue eyes. What he saw filled his heart with compassion. How would she manage when the cataracts completely clouded her eyes?

He patted her shoulder softly and forced himself to smile. "You have just a start of cataracts, Sena." She looked up at the man with a frown of uncertainty.

"Anything you can do for them, Doc?"

"Well, nothing I can do, but you can work on keeping your eyes healthy so the cataracts do not grow as fast. You need to get plenty of exercise, keep that heart strong. And what you eat can help, too. Carrots are excellent for vision and eye health."

Sena nodded solemnly in thought. "Maybe I can grow my own carrots like I did when Levi was a boy. I will just tuck some seeds in next to the tomato plants." A bright smile lit her face and she turned to leave, her cane clicking a soft rhythm. At the door she stopped and turned her head. "Thank you, kindly, good Doctor. I think you are almost as smart as Doc Evans."

CHAPTER 21

DIGGING FOR VICTORY

"Here you go, Geoffrey. I got all the metal stuff that was not being used." Michael hauled a tin pail out of his wagon and presented it to his neighbor and dear friend just up the road.

"Ah, excellent work, lad! Tin cans, bent nails, broken knife blades." The old gentleman sifted through the contents. "Did you get your mother's permission to remove the metal springs from her clothespins? I see you have an ample supply in here."

"Aw, she won't care. She says we have to do everything we can to help the war effort. Besides, Geoffrey, you said you'd buy new ones to replace them. You know, the pegs without the clasp in the middle?" Michael's hands shaped his description.

"Yes, I have purchased a whole case from Chet that I will gladly trade for the others. I will take a batch to your mother soon." He thanked the boy again and turned to carry the bucket to his pickup.

"Where's Grandpa William?" Michael called out just as the man who had married his grandma walked around the house pushing leather gloves into the back pockets of his striped overalls. "Oh, hey, Grandpa!"

"Good morning, Michael," the man called brightly. "I was just helping your dear grandmother plant her garden. What can I do for you today?"

"I wondered if I could borrow your digging fork and shovel. I am going into town to dig Sena Gullickson's garden bigger." The young boy pushed his boot toe through the dirt and studied the resulting swirl. His eyes were nearly covered by the brown short-brimmed hat that had belonged to his father.

"What a brilliant plan, lad, to help dig Victory Gardens! President Roosevelt has been encouraging Americans to raise more vegetables. He contends it will help with the war effort on the home front by saving more for the troops."

"I don't follow how one little old lady planting some carrots can help win the war!" Bewildered, Michael threw up his hands in then let them fall back to his side.

"I can understand your question, young lad, but please consider. What if thousands or hundreds of thousands of people plant carrots, or a few potatoes and peas? It all adds up to make many meals that don't need to be purchased at stores. That means the vegetables produced by other growers can be shipped to feed our soldiers. Sena's part may seem small, but every little bit helps." William led his grandson to the back yard to find the digging tools.

William proudly laid his hand on the boy's shoulder. "Was this your idea, Michael, to help Sena with her garden?"

"Of course it was my idea. I thought of it just as Lydi said 'you need to go in and dig Sena's garden bigger so she can plant carrots.'" He shoved both hands in his pockets and nodded up to his grandpa with a grin.

"I see. Well done, well done, lad." William chuckled, then offered, "What would you think if I accompanied you? Together we could dig up anyone's garden in Canterbury who needed assistance."

"Oh, wow, that's a better idea!"

"I will dash inside and get my wallet and we will load everything into the pickup." William was almost to the front porch when the wind carried in angry shouting from Michael's home just down the road.

They watched as Anna rounded the corner of the house and spotted her son. She stood, hands on hips, glaring from her back yard, then pointed her finger and yelled, "Michael James Andersson, WHAT HAVE YOU DONE TO MY CLOTHES-PINS?"

The boy drew in a breath, and with wide eyes, turned to the house. At that instant Geoffrey came bounding down the porch steps, package under his arm. Nearly running he headed down the road, calling back to Michael, "No worries, lad. I have it covered."

CHAPTER 22

WAR COVERAGE

"That makes ten quilts to send to the Red Cross for the soldiers," Anna declared as she carefully folded the layers of fabric on the two blankets they had pinned together that morning. "Are you sure we cannot help with the stitching?" She asked as she looked up at her mother and Mae.

Both of the older ladies shook their heads. "No, we have sewing machines. It won't take us long to stitch these tops and backs together. No sense you wasting your time with hand stitches." Mae carried one of the quilts to the back room.

Christina placed the other in her basket to take home. "I am glad to help. It is a small thing we can do for our soldiers."

The group had been meeting in the fabric area of Bellum's Mercantile for several years, cutting and piecing quilts to give away. Louise Bellum was happy to donate remnants from the bolts of fabric she and Chet stocked in the store. She was glad her mother Mae took part in the group. Mae and Christina had become close friends. Lynn Swanson, who with her husband Brad, published the *Canterbury Times-News*, assisted with the cutting and often purchased materials to help with the quilts. She usually brought along the *Des Moines Register* so the group kept up on national news.

Anna folded her hands in front of her and glanced at each of the women sitting around the table. "What would you girls think of sewing a quilt for Sena Gullickson? Lydi said when she and Ethel checked in on Sena she noticed her quilt was threadbare and full of patches."

The others nodded their approval. Louise chimed in, "A wonderful idea, Anna! We can start on that next week. Sena is such a dear old lady, though a bit feisty." Mae and Christina laughed at Louise's comment, but Lynn remained silent.

"Lynn, are you all right? You are unusually quiet today." Anna's concern was obvious as she spoke softly to her friend.

Lynn kept staring at the headlines on the *Register,* "Japanese Smashed at Midway." At last she thoughtfully folded the newspaper, then released her breath with a slow sigh. "Bradley told me last night he wants to enlist." Shock settled over the room. No words were spoken, but the friends' compassion emanated from their faces. "He wants to join the Army Signal Corps, as a reporter and photographer." She shook her head and again stared at the newspaper. "His bright idea is to shoot photos that may be published in *Look* magazine. He knows the editor in Des Moines."

Louise placed her hand over Lynn's. "Do you think as a photographer he might not be in as much danger? Surely he would not be near the front lines of battle!"

Though Louise's words were meant to comfort her friend, Lynn shrugged her shoulders in desolation. "To get the best shots, I would guess they are sent to the places of most action. Besides, there is no safe place for a soldier." Then she emitted a humorless laugh. "He says he will send home all the war news and I can print it, that the *Times* will be the most up-to-date publication in the nation."

Anna swallowed the lump in her throat and quietly addressed her friend. "Lynn, you know we are here for you. If Brad goes overseas, we will help with the paper. Mom and I have always wanted to write anyway." She tried to reassure Lynn with a smile and looked up at her mother, whose eyes were brimming with unshed tears.

Just then the bell over the mercantile door clanged as a man dressed in pin-stripe wool pants and a white shirt entered. He removed his fedora, then strode toward the front desk where Chet stood and accepted the man's outstretched hand.

"I don't know if you remember me, Chet. I'm Josiah Masters." The man saw a look of recognition pass over Chet Bellum's face. "I hope you don't hold it against me, Chet. I know I owed you money, but we lost the farm back in 1937 and I did not have one penny to my name. No rain. No crops. I kept the bills and promised myself that as soon as I could I would come back and make things right with you."

Chet waved both hands in front of him, as if to dismiss any hard feelings. "I remember you now, Josiah, but you don't have to pay that bill. A lot of people couldn't pay their bills and they just moved away. Louise and I did just fine. Don't you worry about that money now."

Josiah placed a sealed envelope on the counter. "No, Chet, I want to pay you. I'm just sorry it took so long. There's eighteen dollars in there. $17.20

for what I owe and the rest for interest. That should cover it, as well as my conscience." His mouth turned up in a smile of satisfaction. He shook Chet's hand again, tipped his hat to the women at the back table and walked out the door.

Slowly the storekeeper reached for the envelope and ripped it open. He dumped the money and the yellowed bill stubs on the counter and stared for a few seconds. Finally, he slumped down in his chair. Astonished that anyone would return to pay a bill from more than five years ago, he looked up at Lynn as he spoke. "All we hear about is war. We need more happy stories about good, honest people--like that man."

CHAPTER 23

BECKY

Had Doctor Gus seen her blush? Lydi was certain there was a twinkle in his eyes when he asked her to walk to Hindricks' Pharmacy to purchase supplies for the examination room cabinet. Her heart sang at the prospect of seeing Benjamin.

List in hand, the girl started for the door, then realized she was leaving the doctor without help. She turned back. "Do you want me to wait until Becky comes in? Someone may come in for an appointment.

The doctor's dark brows turned down in a glint of worry as he glanced toward the door that led to the Evans family home. "No, you run along, Lydi.

Maybe little Mary Ann is still sleeping. I will be fine on my own."

Benjamin was arranging the display of *Smith Brothers* cough drops when the pharmacy door chimed. "Hi, Lydi!" His face lit with a welcoming smile.

Willing her heart to stop pounding, she explained what Doctor Gus needed and handed him the paper. Promising to return immediately, Ben hurried to the back room where his father was filling prescriptions.

In a few minutes he hastened back into the room. Before anyone could walk in and ruin his opportunity, Benjamin blurted, "Lydi, may I walk you home tonight after work?"

Taken by surprise, her eyes flew to his. "Oh! Umm. You don't have to do that. It is out of the way for you. We go by your house, so you will have to walk back home." What was wrong with her? She was spluttering worse than a child!

Benjamin shrugged and replied with a grin, "That's the idea, isn't it?"

Lydi did not remember one thing about her stroll back to the doctor's surgery. Every word Benjamin said ran through her mind over and over. Her excitement transferred to the door and the bell clamored wildly. "Oh. Sorry!" She flushed again as she saw the doctor walk away with a perceptive smirk.

At that moment Becky padded in quietly, carrying Mary Ann on her left hip and sliding an envelope into her apron pocket. She set the child down next to the toy box, then, without a sound, stepped behind the counter and began to arrange papers.

People came in, spoke with Becky and then waited in chairs around the outside of the room until Lydi called their names. The time passed quickly as she found charts, guided patients into the examination room and helped with cleanup after each appointment. At last the final patients filed out the front door.

Becky looked tired and her toddler was beginning to fuss. The woman welcomed Lydi's offer to care for the child. Lydi sat on the floor with Mary Ann on her lap. Soon both were stacking wooden blocks. The baby quickly learned to push the stack over, resulting in a crash and a giggle. Lydi smiled and looked up at Becky.

The young woman sat at the desk staring down at what looked like a letter, though her face was devoid of any emotion. Her husband had sent several letters. He was stationed at an emergency medical services hospital in Bristol, England. It was a 600-bed facility, but already there had been times when they had to set up extra cots in the halls. The facility was crowded with injured soldiers, and more were carried in every day. Paul said they already had a shortage of bandages. He asked how she and Mary Ann were doing? Had their baby learned any new words? His last comments were how much he missed them and he just knew her letters must have been lost or held up somewhere. He could not wait to hear from her.

Becky's eyes filled with tears. She had tried to write to her husband many times. She asked about his safety. She wrote about Mary Ann, how she loved to open the kitchen cupboards, and pull everything out, how she giggled at the silliest things. Always at this point in her letters, her thoughts turned to what weighed most heavily on her mind. She could not tell him about that, not yet. So, she crumpled the paper and threw it away. There were no lost letters; she had not sent any.

Tired of the blocks, the baby crawled to the basket of books. "Shall we read a book?" Lydi asked and held out her hands as the child reached for her. They settled in the rocking chair and were soon lost in the *Tale of Peter Rabbit*. The rhythm of the words and the soft sway of the chair relaxed them both and soon little Mary Ann's eyelids were drooping. She snuggled closer to her caretaker and her tiny hand closed on Lydi's thumb. Fondly, the young girl enveloped the child's hand in her own.

Her smile was snuffed out by the cold, empty stare that met her when she glanced up at the baby's mother. A chill ran down Lydi's spine. She had never seen the young woman in such a state. Uncomfortable, Lydi shifted in the chair and quietly set the book aside, then rose to take the child to her mother. She barely heard the words, spoken in a raspy whisper. "At least Mary Ann has you, Lydi."

CHAPTER 24

WALKING HOME

Her shyness vanished like the bright sun over the horizon as Lydi walked home with Benjamin at her side. He talked about his family and his father's plan for him to take over the family pharmacy someday. Lydi peeked over at her friend. "Is that what you want to do?"

"I am not sure, Lydi. Some days I think it would be a good thing. Pharmacists are certainly needed." He hesitated for a few seconds, then released a long sigh. "Lately, I have been thinking I want to work more closely with patients. Would it bother you if I told you I also would like to become a doctor?"

"Of course not, Benjamin! I could definitely see you as a doctor, and a very good one." She smiled, then turned her eyes to the road before them. Where would he go to college? Medical School? Lydi wanted to know, but she did not think it was right to ask. The thought of not seeing him for months or years made her feel empty inside.

Suddenly, she remembered Becky's strange behavior and, to her own amazement, felt comfortable talking to him about what had happened that afternoon. "She seems so sad and withdrawn. I get the idea she does not want to talk to anyone." Lydi lifted her hands in frustration as she finished voicing her thoughts.

Benjamin considered Lydi's sentiments as the Andersson barn came into view. "It must be difficult to raise a baby all alone. I am sure Becky misses her husband."

"Yes, of course," Lydi agreed. "But I think she may have struggled with times of sadness and anxiety even before the war. When I first began working with Dr. Evans, he told me he needed to bring his wife home from Chicago. He seemed concerned that she might not want to leave her mother."

"My dad has talked about this," Benjamin added with a thoughtful frown, "how people feel helpless and alone even though they are surrounded by others. He says some cannot cope with their sadness."

"I am sure things will get better when Dr. Evans comes home." Lydi tried to insert a positive note, but could not help adding, "I sometimes wish he would not have enlisted."

They were nearing Lydi's house. Benjamin stopped and turned to face the girl he adored. "It is what men must do when there is a war going on." A fleeting shadow of regret flashed across his eyes.

"So you will enlist when you turn 18 if the war continues?" Something twisted in Lydi's heart as he nodded silently. Fervently, she prayed that the war would end before then.

CHAPTER 25

DARKNESS

Lydi had nearly turned down her mother's offer of a ride home today after work. She hoped that Benjamin might ask to walk her home again. Later, noticing an ominous cloud approaching from the west, the girl was glad she would have a ride.

The bell over the outside door clanked dully as the last patients called their goodbyes. Most came for follow-up exams and checkups. The one emergency call was Arden Feldman who had stepped on a nail in the back yard and needed a tetanus shot. Dr. Gus strolled out of his office, hands in his pockets, whistling a happy tune. "Thank you to my very capable office assistants," he said as he smiled at Lydi, then turned to Becky. "Becky, please tell your good husband when you write him that when he comes back there will be a slew of babies for him to take care of."

With a smile Lydi looked up at the young woman, but Becky remained silent, staring blankly at a spot on the desk in front of her. Lydi wondered at the woman's strange behavior. As she had confided in Benjamin the day before, Becky seemed to withdraw more into herself each day.

Concern flashed in the doctor's eyes as he glanced at the woman at the desk. He stared at the floor for a few seconds. At last he drew in a breath and glanced at his pocket watch. "If you girls will be all right, I think I will head for home before the storm hits."

Lydi gave the doctor a quick nod and continued picking up the books and toys that had been strewn around the children's table in the waiting room. Soon after the man had left, a gloomy darkness descended upon them. It was as dark as night.

She flipped on the switch for the overhead bulb, but even then the heavy blackness prevailed. Not a single bit of light shone through the front windows. Fear clenched in Lydi's heart as she tried to peer out into the darkness.

A distant flash of lightning brightened the room for just a moment and five seconds later a bolt of thunder crashed so near and loud that Lydi jumped and let out a small cry. She peered quickly up at Becky, but still the woman stared as if in a trance.

In the room next door Mary Ann began to cry, awakened by the deafening crash. Lydi waited, expecting the child's mother to go to her, but she did not move, nor did the expression on her face change. The baby's cries became more and more frantic. Finally, Lydi spoke to Becky. "Shall I go get Mary Ann, Becky? Can I help?"

By now the cries had intensified to panicked screams. How can she ignore her child's cries?

Lydi wondered. Worry overcame her, for surely something was terribly wrong. Even as the young girl walked to the Evans' apartment door, Becky remained like a statue. Lydi found the child's crib and rushed to her. The baby's arms reached up and Lydi held her close, rubbing her back and speaking in soft, soothing tones. Soon the cries diminished to breathy sobs that shook her tiny body every few seconds. Finally, the child calmed enough for Lydi to lay her gently back on the bed and quickly change her wet diaper, struggling to keep the child still enough to safely secure the large pins. Again the child reached for her and Lydi carried Mary Ann back to the waiting room, hoping that seeing her child would revive the woman. An empty chair behind the counter shouted a silent warning. Becky was gone! Terror consumed Lydi and her heart pounded wildly. Had the child's mother gone out into the storm?

She called out, struggling to keep the panic from her voice, "Becky! Becky, where are you?" The black portent still loomed outside the window. Lydi kept calling as she considered where the woman could have gone. Her eyes flew to the door of the examination room. It stood partly ajar.

With the child still in her arms she cautiously pushed through the opening. Becky stood there next to the medicine cabinet. Her eyes were fixed on something she held in her hands, a brown glass bottle. A bottle full of white pills.

Mary Ann tried to reach out. "Mama!" The mother's head remained bent toward the bottle. She stood there, still as stone. It was as though she had not heard her child's plea.

Suddenly the stark, sickening realization hit Lydi like a blow to her stomach.

CHAPTER 26

BECKY'S REVELATION

"You and Mary Ann can stay here as long as you want, Becky." Anna gently reached out to touch the woman's hands that were folded in front of her, watching for any kind of reaction. She looked frail, thin and empty as she sat at the small kitchen table, eyes unfocused.

The teakettle on the front burner of the wood-stove began to steam, and Anna stood to pour boiling water over the green leaves that awaited in the tea pot. She brought cups and saucers from the cupboard and gently placed them on the table. As the tea steeped she studied the woman, seemingly entombed in grief.

Out of nowhere a gust of wind slammed against the north side of the house, and rain pounded loudly on the roof. Then, a deafening clap of thunder, a twin to the one that had shattered the silence at the clinic, crashed close by.

Fear shot into Becky's eyes and she stood, wildly searching the blackness outside the window. "Mary Ann! Where is Mary Ann?" she yelled desperately and turned to the outside door.

Anna rushed to her side and gently put her arms around her shoulders. "Mary Ann is upstairs with Lydi. She is fine. Just fine." She pulled her closer and rubbed her hand down her back, speaking softly.

Becky's eyes met Anna's and suddenly she threw her arms around her friend, leaned into her, and she began to cry. Immense sobs convulsed her body, and Anna felt wetness soak through her dress. She stood for a long time while her young friend's head shuddered against her neck. A glimmer of light peeked into the window as the perilous clouds scudded into the distance.

At last, after the dam of tears had emptied, without lifting her head, Becky spoke in a hoarse whisper. "I don't know if I can do this, Anna." She drew in a huge breath and Anna felt the woman's head shake in desolation.

"We are here if you need us, Becky." She forced herself to smile, hoping that it would convey hope. "The war won't go on forever. That man of yours will be coming home before you know it!"

Slowly, pulling away from Anna's hug, Becky sniffed and lifted her eyes. "It is not just that. Many women have husbands in the war. I think I could deal with that."

A light pattering sounded from the ceiling above them. Lydi's muted voice wafted down the steps, followed by a toddler's giggle.

Becky reached up to massage her forehead, her eyes clouded with worry. Then she hung her head and softly whispered, "Oh, Anna, I am pregnant."

CHAPTER 27

GRANDMA'S SECRET MISSION

It was Sunday afternoon. A gentle breeze brushed the living room curtains and carried in the cheerful twitter of goldfinches as they flitted through the maple tree next to the house. Mom's knitting needles clicked out a small pair of navy blue socks; it seemed Michael wore them out faster than she could knit them. *Pride and Prejudice* rested in Lydi's lap, her head bent, totally absorbed in the story. Michael sat at the living room table carving a sheep, larger than his usual. The slivers of wood fell to the surface. Mary Ann sat on her mother's lap on the davenport, chattering happily as she hugged one of Lydi's old dolls.

There was a light knock on the back door, then subsequent clicks as it opened and shut. "It's me!" Grandma Christina called and then came parading breathlessly into the dining room. She placed a large wicker basket on the table, then gave each of her grandkids and her daughter a quick hug as she greeted them. She patted Becky's shoulder and bent to speak to baby Mary Ann as though their presence at her daughter's was nothing unusual at all.

"Did you bring food?" Michael eyed the basket and sniffed, hopefully.

Grandma laughed brightly. "Always thinking about your stomach, Michael! No, I just thought I would bring quilt blocks over. I have had a time keeping up with pinning and sewing all the blocks we cut for quilts and was hoping for some extra hands." Lydi set aside her book and went to sit next to her grandmother. Anna followed, the corners of her mouth turned up just a bit.

"Our little sewing group at Chet's store has made a bunch of blankets to ship, but I just keep thinking they need more." She swiftly spread out stacks of fabric squares and produced two pincushions from the bottom of her basket, loaded with shiny pinheads.

Becky, who had remained silent as the others gathered at the table, peeked back at the group as they lined up blocks and began pinning them together. She spoke quietly to Mary Ann and set her down on the living room rug with a stack of toys. With hesitant steps she soon stood behind the empty chair. "Can I help, Christina?"

"Oh, of course, Becky. You just sit right down. If I'd known you were here, I would have brought a bunch more blocks," Grandma replied nonchalantly and turned her eyes back to her work. Lydi frowned slightly and peeped up at her mother. She had slipped out early this morning and informed Grandma, William, and Geoffrey that Becky would be staying for a while and why. Grandma was as honest as the day was long. Why would she pretend she did not know the situation? Mom gave Lydi a quick wink and realization dawned on her. She hid her smile, but memories of the grief Mom had endured after Dad died flashed through the young girl's mind. Grandma had made sure Anna knew she was needed even when she had withdrawn to her bed, numbed with grief. The old woman possessed an uncanny talent for healing broken hearts.

The five worked in companionable silence while strips of pinned squares grew in the basket. Christina chattered about the scrap drives and how her husband and Geoffrey had hauled three loads of metal to Council Bluffs. The metal would go into building war tanks and planes. Then she said that Mae and Louise had five more bolts of fabric that Chet ordered on sale, so there would be more cutting to do at the store, more quilts to make. "William says everything we do on the home front helps win the war. Why, if I found out soldiers were doing without anything over there, I would never forgive myself for not trying to help." She focused on her pinning.

Becky had sat working quietly, occasionally checking to make sure Mary Ann was safe where she played. At Christina's comment about soldiers doing without, her hands stopped and for several seconds the woman remained still as stone, staring at a spot on the table. She frowned in deep thought, slowly lay the blocks down and reached into her skirt pocket. Lydi, who sat next to her, waited for Becky to produce something from her pocket, but she only touched whatever was there, her hand remaining still in the folds. Suddenly her expression softened and she spoke quietly. "Bandages. The soldiers need bandages. Paul said they don't have enough at the hospital."

Becky did not notice Christina's satisfied smile, but Lydi and her mom did.

CHAPTER 28

ORPHANS

"Mom! Grandma! Come, quick!" Michael called frantically as he burst in the front door. Tears streamed down his fear-filled face. He nestled a small black form close to his chest while his right hand stroked softly over its side. A soft dark feather twirled to the floor as a sob tremored from the boy's body.

Anna rushed to her son's side. "What is it? What is wrong, Michael?"

"It's Little Black Banty." He gently laid his head against the small hen as his eyes squeezed shut in pain. "She's hurt bad." His mother wrapped the boy in a hug as she reached to touch the animal. Her heart hurt for her son, and as much as she wanted to shield him from life's sorrows, she knew she could not. Grandma Christina stood next to them, her heart wrenching at the sight. He sniffed and ran his sleeve under his nose, all the while caressing his treasure. Becky looked on quietly from the couch.

"I heard her squawking outside the barn when I was milking AmyBelle. I ran outside and there was a big old bobcat chasing after her. It ran away when it saw me, but when I got to her she was just lying in the grass." The child shook his head and his eyes filled again as he hugged the lifeless body. "She died trying to protect her babies."

Anna's eyes flew to her mother's. Each year the little hen managed to steal a nest and eventually emerged leading a small flock of chicks. They imagined the carnage the boy may have seen following the bobcat's attack.

Suddenly the door opened again and with it a cacophony of frenzied peeping. Lydi was carrying a feed bucket. Through her tears she managed a slight smile. Then she held the bucket up. "There are five, and they look like their mama."

Becky stood then, drawn to the frantic babies. She looked into the pail as Lydi held it up. The woman reached in and touched the soft downy head of a tiny black chick. "Will they live?" She asked, turning to search Christina's face.

With a great sigh, the older woman peered in the bucket. "It's hard to tell," she speculated thoughtfully. "They are pretty young and babies do need their mama." She let the words steep for a few seconds, then pulled her grandchildren close. "Let's go give Little Black Banty a proper burial, then we will see what can be done for the chicks. As the door clicked behind them, Becky stared into the pail as the calls became more desperate. "Babies need their mama," she whispered.

Twenty minutes later Michael kicked off his chore boots in the back porch as he and Lydi, Mom and Grandma returned. The four froze in place at the sight before them as they entered the kitchen. Baby Mary Ann stood peeking over the side of the wood box, her chubby hands reaching down. Her mother kneeled next to her, speaking softly as her arms moved, working with something in the box. Soft twittering sounds rose from the box. Mary Ann giggled.

Becky glanced up at the family who had taken her in. Then she pulled herself up and reached for her child. "I hope it was all right to bring the chicks in here, close to the stove. I assumed they should be kept warm." Her eyes were soft and bright. "I heated your irons on the stove, Anna, and wrapped them in Mary Ann's old diapers."

The four moved in close and were soon on their knees, amazed at the scene in the wood box. White swaddled masses formed a half circle over a soft baby blanket in a corner. Cuddled together on the blanket were five balls of fluff. Three had tucked their heads under their wing. The others snuggled up next to their siblings.

Michael managed a wobbly smile and patted Mary Ann's head. "I think they are going to make it." He looked up. "Thanks, Becky."

CHAPTER 29

WINNING THE BATTLE

A light knock on the front door startled Becky out of her intent concentration. Lately, when Mary Ann napped, she had been drawn to the family Bible that rested on the lamp table next to the davenport. Reverently, she replaced it, and still in thought about the reading, walked to the door.

"Good morning, Mrs. Evans." William bowed politely and managed to remove his hat though his arms were full. She nodded a smile to this man who always seemed to emanate kindness. He shifted slightly in the doorway and looked down at the white bundle in his arms. "I brought a bolt of fabric that would work for bandages. Chet at the mercantile had it in the back room. Christina mentioned that your good husband declared a need for wound dressings."

A slight glimmer of realization lit her eyes. "Oh, yes! Forgive me. Please come in."

The old gentleman placed the fabric on the dining room table. "Christina and I will stop over after supper tonight and help with cutting and rolling. You would know what the doctor needs at his hospital."

The woman still seemed wrapped in her thoughts as she stared at the white layers as the front door closed with a gentle click. Her hands reached for the soft material and her fingertips smoothed the gauzy folds. She reached in her pocket to touch what rested there. Then she smiled.

That night after supper when Christina and William came to visit they found Michael on the living room floor playing with little Mary Ann. She was holding a wooden sheep he had carved. Laughter floated from the kitchen and soon Lydi, Anna and Becky came to greet their beloved guests.

With a proud grin, Becky's gaze turned to the stack of bandages in the middle of the table, neatly rolled and fastened with safety pins. Anna wrapped an arm around the young mother's shoulders, but her twinkling eyes met her mother's.

That night, when Mary Ann was tucked safely in bed, Rebecca Evans wrote her husband a very long letter. This time she mailed it.

CHAPTER 30

BILLIE COMES THROUGH

The clip-clop of approaching hooves made Lydi look back as she started her walk home from the doctor's office in Canterbury. It was Ethel on School Boy Bill! The gentle horse trotted up and stopped next to Lydi as she waited to hug her dear friend.

"Oh, Lydi, it is so good to see you! I got a letter from Billie and if I had known, I would have brought it." Ethel led Bill as she walked next to her friend.

"Well, just tell me what she wrote," Lydi entreated as the girls shuffled over the rutted road.

Ethel grinned at Lydi's excitement. "Her friends, the Japanese family that was forced to go to Camp Amache, are doing well. The girls' father is in charge of building more facilities at the camp. Akito and Yuna and their mother are helping dig up sod ground to be planted next year. They are hoping to raise vegetables and grain to feed the other internment camps.

Lydi looked relieved as her eyes focused in the distance. "That is good. Even though it is sad that they had to move out of their homes, they are making the best of their situation."

Ethel continued. "Billie's sister, Dru, got a job at a war materials factory in Boulder. She makes almost as much money as their father working in the mines!"

"Wow!" Lydi exclaimed. "I read in the Des Moines paper that women are taking over jobs in almost every factory. They have to since there are not enough men left here in the U.S."

"That is just what Billie said." Ethel turned to her friend. "There are so many women going to work that Dru told Billie they needed someone to babysit the children. Billie said she thought about it and decided that her moping around about the war being stupid was not doing any good, so she decided to start a day care business!"

"That is just perfect for Billie," Lydi interjected. "She is good with youngsters and so fun-loving. I can just see her directing plays and skits with the little ones singing and reciting verses."

"Funny, that is almost exactly what she wrote!" Ethel laughed and the girls strode on in lighthearted banter until Lydi's barn came into view.

The girls hugged goodbye, thankful that their paths had crossed.

Ethel climbed back up on her trusty steed and grinned at her friend. "We will see each other again soon. Every day. School starts in just a couple weeks."

Lydi smiled at the thought. Just two more years and she would be ready to begin pre-medical school. She had not thought about it much lately. It seemed like the war had even made her forget her dream.

CHAPTER 31

GETTING THE NEWS OUT

The bell jangled happily over the door at the *Canterbury Times-News* office. Becky Evans swept in, juggling little Mary Ann on her left hip. She smiled at the three women as they worked, Lynn and Anna at the linotype and Christina at the desk. Becky set a small stack of papers in front of Christina. "Here is my article for next week. I hope it helps."

Lynn looked up, eyes shining. "Helps? Becky, since your weekly stories have been printed, Chet says the donations for the war effort have tripled! It helps."

"Thank you for the kind words, Lynn. It does seem right to be doing something and feel that I might be making a difference, even in a small way." The young mother looked down at her child thoughtfully, then her expression turned serious and a worried frown creased her brows. "What have you heard from Brad?"

Lynn sighed wistfully and placed another block of type letters into the printing machine. "Well, he writes almost every day." She paused a few seconds and finally shook her head. "I've been married to that man for nearly eight years, long enough to know when he is keeping something from me. I guess you could say I try and read between the lines."

Christina paused in her writing and her eyes met Lynn's. "William says soldiers are not allowed to give out any information that might endanger people or military actions. It could be that Brad is sworn to secrecy or he knows his letters will be censored. If missions or locations get in the wrong hands, there could be devastating losses."

"Yes, I have thought of that," Lynn spoke as she worked, "but it is ironic that the man, a born photographer and reporter, joined the military to get the news back to the States and then he cannot even write to his wife about what he is doing or where he is stationed."

Anna, whose heart still ached at the loss of her own husband, understood worry and grief. She pulled both of the young wives into a warm embrace. "I know you cannot help but worry about them, but you are doing the best you can here at home. I am sure Brad is proud of the paper that you are putting out, Lynn. And Becky, I bet your husband brags to the other doctors how his wife is sending bandages and supplies." She stepped back and smiled at her friends. "Someday, they will be able to tell you all their stories."

CHAPTER 32

UNREVEALED SECRETS

The glare of the sun over the vast expanse of water almost blinded him as he peered out over the wing of the British aircraft. Gradually, gentle rolling hills materialized and the water along the shoreline transformed to a luminous cerulean that reminded him of Lynn's tear-filled eyes the day he told her goodbye. How he missed her. How he wanted to write her every detail of the flights, the missions, the people and their secrets.

Bradley Swanson clenched his jaw until his teeth hurt. He was a journalist. Writing is what he lived for, but his dreams of covering the war, photographing the action and sending it all to his wife back in Canterbury had been destroyed the moment he was sworn to secrecy. No detail, photo or location could be revealed. "Loose lips sink ships," they forewarned. Letters would be censored.

"We will soon be there, mate." The pilot grinned. "I'll get her down close for maybe four seconds, but we'll have to ascend fast." A gray precipice loomed in the shadows, below which the forms of ships swelled as they grew closer. Brad readied his camera and held his breath as the night fighter plane plummeted.

He shot four quick shots of the ships in the harbor, hoping they would be clear in spite of the plane's vibration. Doubtful that he would ever find out, he snapped a few more photos of the nearby terrain and the ships moving out to sea. Fred, the pilot, would fly them back to London where Brad had strict instructions to turn in the film and wait for his next assignment.

The light aircraft, a British de Havilland Mosquito, responded to Fred's touch like a kitten as he eased her up, almost brushing the mountain. He lovingly patted the instrument panel in front of him. "Grand work, Maude!" Then he dipped the fighter plane into a nose-dive on the other side of the mountain and leveled it with a tailspin before accelerating to 600 kilometers per hour for their trip "home." He slapped Brad's knee. "Just making sure you change your boxers, lad!" The man threw back his head and laughed uproariously. Brad just shook his head, imagining what a colorful character Fred would be in a story, but not a story he could tell.

He could not write home about the reason he took the photos, the radio messages transcribed in secret code. He could not tell anyone about the code breakers. The gruff guards surrounding the workers would not allow a photograph. During his one brief glimpse into a large noisy room in Bletchley Park, he observed hundreds of women. Some clicked away at small machines. Several women gathered around the desk of a worker in the corner, cheering her on. Their role was to decipher coded messages from Japanese and German vessels. Once locations and tactics were revealed, Fred and Brad were given their assignment. Fred maneuvered "Maude" to the site. Brad snapped pictures.

Fred informed Brad that more than 9,000 code-breakers were enlisted at the Bletchley Mansion in England. In the United States a similar group, also mostly women, worked in Washington, D.C. Together they were cracking the secrets of German and Japanese wartime communication.

Brad's work was classified. Top secret. No details could be sent home to Lynn, but in the meantime, the stories clicked through his brain like the linotype printer, and he imagined how his wife's bright blue eyes would sparkle when he finally could tell her.

CHAPTER 33

MILKWEED MANIA

"What's that pointy thing on my desk, Miss Bollinger, with the stuffing coming out of it?" Vicky Christleton inquired as she returned to the classroom after noon recess, smelling of sunshine, fresh October air, and child.

"It is a milkweed pod, Vicky. Our lesson and project for this afternoon are all about milkweeds." The teacher smiled as each student began to examine the prickly shell. When all were settled in their places, she reached for a dry stalk with several pods attached. Tiny wisps of fluff stuck to dark seeds escaped into the air and landed throughout the room.

"You have probably seen milkweed plants growing around the schoolyard, in fence lines and ditches," the instructor began. "Some people consider them pests and weeds, but right now, during the war, they are very valuable."

The children ran their fingers over the rough outer coating and rubbed the white silky strands between their fingers as they listened and learned. Each pod contains around 400 fibers attached to 170 seeds. The plant comes up wild in the spring, produces a large blossom made up of many small pink flowerets. The bees and butterflies love the nectar in the flowers. Eventually the flowers dry up and pods are formed on the plant. The plump dry pods split open when the seeds are ripe. It is at this time that the plant is so useful.

Her eyes swept over her students and her heart swelled with pride. Since the war began, they were willing to do everything possible to help on the home front. She knew the milkweed project would be no exception.

"Have you ever tossed a cork into a bucket of water?" she asked. "What does the cork do?"

Emma raised her hand immediately to answer. "It floats. Even if you push it down and hold it under, it pushes right back up."

"Excellent answer, Emma. Cork floats. It is extremely buoyant, and just like Emma said, it pushes right back up to the surface of the water." The youngsters' eyes followed the teacher as she walked among them. "Milkweed fluff is even more buoyant than cork. It is coated with a thin layer of oil which helps it stay dry and float. Think about what might be needed by our soldiers that floats." The teacher watched as several hands went up.

Ricky's face beamed brightly and Miss Bollinger could not resist learning his answer.

"Boats! I bet the soldiers need a lot of boats that float in the ocean," he replied as he searched for affirmation.

"Yes, it is true that soldiers need boats to float," the young woman nodded. "What other things can you think of that might be needed to make something or someone float? Maybe something the soldiers might wear?"

Mr. Hindricks, Adam and Benjamin's father, had read his family an article about the milkweed processing plant in Petoskey, Michigan. He had told his sons about the war uses of the fibers in the plant. Adam Hindricks raised his hand to answer the teacher's question. "Life jackets. The milkweed sewn into them helps keeps soldiers afloat when they need to swim to shore or out to a boat." His young face grew serious as he added, "Or if their plane gets shot down over the ocean."

"Good, Adam. The milkweed threads are also used in sleeping bags and parachutes to keep them afloat whenever needed." Radio news broadcasts often reported the most mortifying incidents. The teacher was aware of what was flashing through many of her students' imaginations and she hoped to avoid exacerbating the cloud of doom that seemed to hover since the war began. "Tons of milkweed pods are needed, and possibly we can help."

"Are we gonna go pick some?" Vicky's eyes lit at the prospect of helping.

"Yes, Vicky, but first we need to know what we are looking for. Only the ripe pods like those on your desks should be harvested. You will know that they are ready as they split open and the silky threads begin to push out. The seeds attached must be brown, or the material cannot be used for the floating devices."

Miss Bollinger strode back to her desk to a stack of cloth bags. "We will collect the milkweed pods in these, and Mr. Bellum at the mercantile will bring a special bag used for drying them. Full bags will be shipped to the plant in Michigan that Adam mentioned."

Two hours later, twenty-two bags were partly filled. The next week the teacher was presented with that many more almost every morning.

CHAPTER 34

PUTTING ON AIRS

Gertrude Niggle was dreading the next two hours of her life. Her husband had been tormenting her for some time about spending time with his boss's wife. She had reminded him that back before little Laurene was born, she had learned who her true friends were. "I refuse to put on airs to impress anyone, Mort. Money and fancy clothes don't mean everything,"

"Well, money may not mean everything to you, but it puts food on the table. And it buys Laurene's dresses." He let that sink in. "I'm up for a promotion in January, but Benson might just pass me up for one of the younger guys. Their wives are all friends, you know. Couldn't you invite Babette

173

out for coffee, just once?" She had felt the annoyance in his tone. She had extended the invitation.

The knock on the door made her stomach twist in knots. The woman glanced in her daughter's room where Laurene was tugging the dress off her baby doll. Then she drew in a fortifying breath, pasted on a smile and opened the door. "Hello, Babette. Please come in."

"Oh, Gertie, it is SO good to see you! It's been a while." The guest looked down at the floor and eased in hesitantly, as if she might step in something unpleasant. She scanned the room. Was that mockery in her eyes? "Your little house is so, ummm, comfortable," she gushed as she slipped the cashmere sweater off her shoulders and paraded to the davenport.

Following behind her, Gert noticed the perfectly straight lines running down each of Babette's legs, and blurted out, "You still have nylon stockings? All the women around Canterbury donated ours to the war effort."

"Hmph! There is no way I am giving up my stockings for some silly old parachute. Fashion is just too important." She crossed her long legs as she sat and patted her hair that flipped up at the bottom. Then she tugged at the waist of her skirt. "I hate these new corsets. Instead of elastic they have to use whale bones. Rubber is in short supply and the government is using it for jeep tires and other silly war materials. Little is left for elastic, so they use whale bones instead. That is the most ridiculous thing I have ever heard of. I told my husband yesterday he was going to order me an elastic corset, I didn't care how much it cost!" She smiled coyly to herself and studied her polished nails. "And he will."

Gert thought of their son, Lem, who was stationed in Africa, Private First Class. His letters revealed that he was happy in the army. He loved seeing new places and the camaraderie he felt with the other soldiers. Lem was thinking he might make it his career. Her son had matured in the service and outgrown his youthful rebellion. Now he was determined to help win the war, no matter what the cost.

The young mother wanted to tell the selfish person next to her that every sacrifice was worth it if it helped win the war, helped save lives. Helped save her son. She pursed her lips to keep the words from pouring out.

Just then Laurene toddled into the room dragging her doll that was naked except for shoes and white lace socks. She stared at Babette, circling far around her to get to her mother. "Mommy," she said quietly as she crawled onto her lap.

Babette scowled at the child. "I don't know why you ever had a baby when Lem was nearly grown. You could have been free," she added, nodding disdainfully at Laurene, "from that." She reached in her tan leather purse and pulled out a cigarette case. Without asking, she lit one, inhaled and blew the smoke out evenly, looking up at the ceiling.

As tendrils of gray-white vapor reached the child, she wrinkled her nose and fanned her hand in front of her face to dash it away. "Pew! It stinks, Mommy."

Rolling her eyes, Babette faked a smile and patted Laurene's doll. "Why don't you and your dolly go somewhere else?" Quickly, she pulled her hand away and stared down at it, with a look of total revulsion. She wiped her palm on the couch.

Gert leaped to her feet, thinking Mort would not be happy with her. "I'll bring some coffee, Babette. You just wait right there." She took Laurene back to her room. "You play in here for a bit, then Mommy will come find you." She lovingly patted her daughter's soft curls and headed for the kitchen.

The conversation turned to their husbands and the lumberyard. How business had picked up since the war began and the demand for metals and wood had skyrocketed. Babette smugly declared that their son would not be drafted, that his father had made a little visit with the gentleman at the draft board and convinced him that the boy was needed to work at the business. She patted Gertrude's hand and confided with a smirk, "Money talks, you know."

The afternoon seemed to drag on forever for Gertrude Niggle. Finally, her guest looked at her watch pin and announced that it was time for her to go home. She stood and pulled her sweater over her shoulders. She opened the door and then turned back to her hostess, "Thank you for entertaining me."

Gert forced a smile and hoped that Babette did not hear the sarcasm in her voice. "Oh, you are so welcome, Babette."

CHAPTER 35

LOST!

"Wait! What was that noise?" Benjamin and Lydi were nearly to the end of her driveway when Lydi thought she heard someone yelling. They stopped. Suddenly the voice came again. "It's Mrs. Niggle," said Lydi, "and she is calling for Laurene." They listened intently, and this time the shout seemed closer, clearer. "She sounds frantic. Laurene must be lost!"

For a split second their eyes met, and though they spoke no words, both knew what they needed to do. Benjamin tore down the road to the Niggle's home. Lydi tossed her school things onto the porch and called to her mother before pursuing her dear friend. It would soon be dark, too dark to find a toddler if she had wandered out into the woods behind the Niggle's house, or into the nearby cornfield. Nights were cold now, far below freezing. Lydi had heard stories of children who had been lost, wandering about in circles. Some were not found until it was too late.

As she ran by Grandma's house, she saw Grandpa William step out of the barn, milk bucket in hand. She yelled that little Laurene must be lost. The old farmer stopped, set down the bucket and turned back to the barn. He put his fingers to his lips and gave one loud, shrill signal. Immediately Romeo came bounding to him and sat, waiting for his command. "He will find her," Grandpa called to Lydi. He made a sign with his hand and pointed. The dog hurtled down the road.

They arrived several minutes behind Benjamin. Mrs. Niggle was pacing back and forth behind her house, wringing her hands. She called her daughter's name, her voice trembling now between sobs. Lydi ran to her and placed a hand on the woman's arm. "Do you have any idea where she may have gone?" Lydi's eyes searched the area.

"No. She has never wandered off by herself. Today I had a visitor. She told Laurie to go away. I thought she had gone to her room and fallen asleep." Gert covered her face with her hands as her whole body shook. "How could I have let this happen?"

"We will find her, Mrs. Niggle. She can't have gone far. Are you sure she is not in the house, maybe hiding somewhere?"

"I checked everywhere. I even went through the barn. She is not here. Benjamin is searching the cornfield." She rubbed her arms with her hands and left them there, as if trying to protect her heart. Fear overtaking her, she peered up at the darkening sky and shook her head in despair.

"Can you find a piece of Laurene's clothing? Or her pillow case? Romeo will find her." Lydi hoped her voice portrayed more confidence than she felt inside.

Gertrude Niggle frowned in confusion; then at once hope flooded back into her soul. She hurried into the house and soon returned, tightly clutching a small pink nightgown. Lydi knelt down next to Romeo with the garment extended. "Romeo, find Laurene." He sniffed and turned his eyes up to Lydi, and she feared for a moment that he did not understand. Then he lifted his nose, turned toward the cornfield and gave a single bark.

The girl followed as the animal headed onto the soft dirt between rows. Lydi struggled to keep up and still tried calling the child's name between deep breaths. On they trudged, deeper and deeper into the tall nearly-brown stalks as the daylight faded and Venus sparkled in the horizon. The rows

seemed to go on forever. Lydi tried peering between the plants on either side, but in the dark she
wondered if she might miss the child if she was lying down or huddled among the bottom corn leaves.
How could they cover every row? Where was Romeo?

She shook herself, troubled by her lack of faith.
A prayer blossomed in her heart and burst forth.
Her feet plodded forward on their own power as the
night became colder and darker.

Suddenly, from far ahead came a short bark
and then a soft whine. Then she heard Benjamin
call. "Lydi, I found her. We are over here."

He kept talking and soon she heard the swish-
ing of the corn leaves as his jeans brushed against
them. Then Romeo emerged and nudged her hand.
He turned back from where he had come and
barked until Benjamin appeared. Laurene's arms
were wrapped tightly around his neck and her legs
around his waist. Her little head snuggled deep into

his neck and every so often she shuddered out a shaky breath.

Benjamin grinned and shook his head. He patted the small child's back and she clutched him even tighter. "I think I have a new friend."

Tears of gratitude filled Lydi's eyes, and at that moment she decided she fell in love with Benjamin Hindricks.

CHAPTER 36

CHRISTMAS BABY

Becky Evans' eyes glistened with happy tears as her husband placed their son on her stomach and prepared to cut the umbilical cord. "You were amazing," he said softly. He clamped the cord, made sure the blood flow had stopped, and severed the connection. Then he wrapped the baby in a soft, cotton, receiving blanket and held him close. Sneezing and fussing a bit, the newborn nuzzled against his father's neck and finally closed his eyes, exhausted.

The woman watched in silence, her heart nearly bursting with thankfulness. Something about a man snuggling a baby tugged at a woman's heart-strings. He nuzzled the top of the child's downy, wet head with his chin, then reverently placed him in his mother's arms.

Dr. Gustavson, who had stood by, ready to assist if needed, cleared his throat and stepped close to the new father. He clapped his back. "You didn't do so bad yourself, 'Dad.'" Beaming, he turned to Becky. "Congratulations, 'Mom.' I am happy for you both."

"I will leave you three alone now," Dr. Gus excused himself, though seeing the couple's silent communication, he wondered if they even heard him. "I will stop at the Andersson's. They will be waiting for the good news, especially Anna."

Paul Evans kept his gaze on his wife and child, and replied softly, "Tell them I will stop in the morning and pick up Mary Ann. She needs to meet her little brother."

Gus picked up his medical bag and padded out of the room. The sound of the front door clicked as it shut behind him.

There was a twinkle in his eyes as the new father sat on the bed. "Do I detect a budding romance between Gus and Anna?"

Becky smiled slightly and feigned a look of innocence. "Far be it from me to reveal my friends' secrets."

Her husband chuckled as his hand rested on hers. "It seems you made a lot of friends while I was away. Lynn and Louise gave me strict orders to keep them informed. Geoffrey, William and Christina fairly paced the floor when Gus told them the baby was coming. Anna, Lydi and Michael have a stack of gifts they have made, ready to deliver the second they can come see you."

"They are like family now. I don't know if I would have made it these last months without all of them." Her brows turned down as she remembered the struggles she endured that summer. She had told her husband everything, first in letters and then again when he came home for Christmas and the birth of their second child. He knew about her sadness and even about the bottle of pills that tempted her to end her life. At the time, when she knew another child had been conceived, she did not think she could bear again the extreme sadness that had descended over her after Mary Ann had been born.

He squeezed her hand and leaned to plant a kiss on her forehead. "Are you worried you will experience the same depression after this birth?" Though he wanted only happy moments for them on this day, he felt it best to be open with each other.

Becky rubbed her fingers over the soft, warm bundle nestled next to her and shook her head in thought. "Life seems different this time. There are so many people who I know will help me. It is as though I have purpose now. Mary Ann is such a joy and the thought of not being here.....I cannot believe I even considered such a dreadful thing." Exhausted, she snuggled deeper into her pillow and closed her eyes. "And now I have faith that God will see me through, no matter what happens. I think we will be all right."

His voice broke with emotion as he looked down at the two miracles before him. "I will be here four more weeks, Becky. We will make the most of every minute."

CHAPTER 37

MEETING OF THE MINDS

"Here, let me hold that big boy," Lynn Swanson cooed, as she reached to take Mack Evans from his mother. She snuggled the baby close and patted his back lightly. Becky noticed the wistful look in her friend's eyes.

"What have you heard from Brad?" Becky inquired as she studied the woman, concerned that she may be succumbing to the constant stress as she worried about her husband who was involved in this never-ending war.

"Oh, the same things. He rides in some kind of fancy light-weight plane with a dare devil pilot. He takes pictures. Of what, he never says. I know he cannot reveal privileged information, Becky, but isn't it ironic that he joined up to send back news and pictures so that we could publish them for the world?" Lynn rolled her eyes in exasperation, then added, "I don't know what to print next week. What news do we have besides the continuous drone about battles?"

Becky sympathized with Lynn. Though she had two young children to occupy her time and energy, she did not have the weekly responsibility of putting out a newspaper. She sat at the long table they sometimes used to line type and picked up a pencil. She tapped it on the table, then tapped the eraser against her chin, thoughts churning. "We could write stories about locals. How different groups are helping on the home front. Make them positive and uplifting in contrast to all the sadness."

Lynn jostled Mack on her shoulder and sat down across from her friend. "That is a great idea! You have been writing about what the soldiers need; now we can fill the paper with all the different groups and their projects. The school kids organized something called 'REACH.' They collected milk weed last fall. Now I believe they are taking turns in visiting families of soldiers. They have been shoveling snow for people in town. If they are given money, they turn it in to Miss Bollinger who is collecting coins for war bonds. Each project could be a positive article."

"We can ask Lydi to help cover the school articles. Maybe Anna and Christina would write about Geoffrey's metal drives. Can you get some photographs?" Becky smiled as her son began to fuss. She reached to take him from Lynn, who was attempting to write notes on a scrap of paper.

"Yes, photos would add to it. We can do that. Thank you, Becky. You are a life-saver."

At that moment, Christina and Anna stepped into the newspaper office, stomped the snow off their boots and smiled at the two sitting at the table.

Anna pulled off her gloves. "You girls look like you are up to trouble. What is going on?"

They apprised the other women of the story ideas, and Anna agreed to interview Geoffrey.

"That reminds me," Becky inserted as her eyes met Christina's. "Paul said when he was home at Christmas that there is a shortage of soap at the hospital. He fretted that the doctors and nurses were not properly scrubbing between patients."

Christina grinned slyly. "Hmmm. I will mention that fact to Geoffrey. That is all it will take."

The four drained the coffee pot that waited on the woodstove in the middle of the large room. Camaraderie and purpose warmed them from the inside. At last, Becky excused herself. "I had better get home. Lydi has other things to do besides watch Mary Ann."

"She is happy to help, Becky," Anna stood to give her friend and her baby a hug. "But, she often tells me how Mary Ann misses her mommy when you leave."

"There is nothing wrong with that," chimed in Christina as she wrapped the warm, hand-knit scarf around her neck. Turning to her daughter, she spoke. "I will visit Mae at the store and be back in two jerks of a lamb's tail. Then we had better get home. We have things to do, places to go and stories to write."

Strolling down the snow packed board walk, Christina smiled and shook her head. "I am beginning to talk like my husband," she thought, and entered the door of the mercantile to ask Mae about more gauze for bandages. *We will win this miserable war yet.*

CHAPTER 38

GEOFFREY DOES IT AGAIN

"I'd go slippery, slippery slidey…" Geoffrey sang a silly soap song as he stirred. His brother William and sister-in-law Christina shook their heads and grinned. The man lived for helping others, especially now during the war. Becky mentioned that her husband, Dr. Paul Evans, lacked good soap for sanitary practices at the war hospital in England.

"When the soap is ready, we will send the lion's share to Dr. Evans in Bristol, England. We will keep some here and give it to families in need." He added a few drops of liquid that made the whole room smell wonderful. Grandma wondered how Geoffrey and William knew so much about so many things. As if in answer, Geoffrey added, "Remember when Mum made soap when we were youngsters, William? She gave it to those who came for healing herbs." Geoffrey smiled wistfully as he always did when speaking of their growing up years.

William nodded. "The process of making soap was much more difficult then. Mum even made her own lye out of wood ashes."

"Yes, we do have it easier now. Chet has caustic soda at the store." Geoffrey stirred and began to hum his song. "We can make more soap when we have more fat. Beef fat is excellent and lard works fine. Two batches will be complete when these dry.

After chores that morning, the old gentleman had pulled out soap-making equipment from the pantry, preparing for his soap-making venture. Christina and William had offered assistance, but Geoffrey insisted on working alone as he gathered large kettles and glass bowls and measures. Over a warm stove he heated the lard and pieces of beef fat to liquid. Then he tied a snow-white handkerchief over his nose and mouth and took the caustic soda and water outside. On a board set over two saw horses, he poured the lye powder into the water. He stood back as far as he could and turned his head while stirring to avoid breathing the exuding fumes. When he felt the solution had cooled in the winter air, he carefully brought it inside to the stove.

"The pleasant sector of the procedure follows." Geoffrey slowly poured the lye solution into the soup pot of fats. He removed the kettle from the stove and stirred, slowly at first, then more rapidly. With the patience of Job, the man stirred for an hour. At last, with beaming face, he turned to the other two. "Come and see. It approaches the molding point."

A thick yellow substance swirled, made waves, and then leveled again with each pass of the spoon.

The consistency reminded Christina of lemon pudding, but this smelled even lovelier, like lavender. She stood back while Geoffrey poured the thick liquid into pans he had lined with parchment. He scraped every possible remnant into the molds.

With a sigh of satisfaction he carried the pans of still-liquid soap into the pantry. Within a few hours it would harden and he would cut it into hand-size bars. Once it cured for a week, the suds would be ready for action.

It is only soap, Geoffrey mused. Could such a trivial thing help win the war? He pictured the good Dr. Evans in the hospital in England. He knew the critical need for cleanliness when fighting infection and disease. Yes, soap could make a difference. As William often said, "Every little bit helps."

CHAPTER 39

RADIO REPORTS

Lydi chopped onions and added them to the meat in the fry pan. The potatoes were boiling. Supper would be ready when Mom came home from her work at the store and the newspaper office. The girl grabbed silverware and three plates from the cupboards and started to the living room table. She stopped short as she saw Michael crouched in front of the Philco radio.

Mom did not approve of them listening when there was work to be done. "You should not be listening now, Michael," Lydi chided. She did not mention that the battery was expensive to replace. Three nights a week and on Saturdays, Mom, Michael and Lydi gathered in their places in front of

199

the device to listen to their favorite programs, *One Man's Family* and *We the People.* Michael loved *The Lone Ranger.*

Tipping her head sideways and turning her ear toward the sound, the girl strained to hear what the announcer was saying. It sounded like he was listing something with a short pause between each item. She shook her head and frowned at the boy for ignoring their mother's wishes. Holding forks just above the table, Lydi opened her mouth to scold her brother, "Michael, I don't think…"

The silverware clattered to the table as she realized her little brother was sobbing. He knelt there, prone, while his entire body shook in desolation. Rushing to his side she dropped to the floor next to him and wrapped her arm around his shoulders. "What is wrong, Michael? Why are you crying?"

She reached to turn the control off and rubbed her hand over the boy's back and shoulders as his young body trembled. Finally he lifted his head and sniffled and rolled back to sit on the floor. "Lydi, it's so sad," he spoke softly, raggedly. "They were naming all the soldiers who died last week." Staring at the floor he shook his head slowly. "What if...what if somebody was listening and they heard their Dad's name? Or their brother's? It would be so awful." At last he looked up at his sister, his face wet with tears.

"Oh, Michael, to lose a loved one in war has to be devastating." Though she was reaching out to comfort her brother, the girl's thoughts were skipping to Becky and Lynn. What if Mabel, Lilly and Julia lost a brother? Though the image lurked in the back of her mind constantly, her heart twisted as she thought, what if Benjamin died in the war? She forced her focus back to Michael's questions and answered. "I think the family is informed first, before the name is announced. An officer brings a telegram to them."

"But, what if they don't know, Lydi? What if there is a mistake and they are sitting in front of their radio and they hear that name?" More tears flowed as Lydi gently pulled her brother to his feet. She wiped his face with her apron and reached for his hand.

"Come, help me set the table and finish supper before Mom comes home." Lydi roused softly as she set the plates around the table.

Michael remained quieter than usual during supper. Anna's questioning eyes met her daughter's. Lydi gave a slight nod, indicating that she knew what was troubling her brother. Finally, Michael spoke. "I'll do supper dishes and you two go listen to *One Man's Family*. I don't feel like hearing it tonight."

"It is all right if you truly don't want to listen, Michael." Mother spoke lightly, though worry creased her brows. "But, if we all work on cleanup tonight, we can have everything done in time. We would like you to listen with us."

"Come on, Michael," Lydi persuaded, hoping the boy would come out of his sadness.

"Oh, I suppose," he sighed as he took his plate to the dishpan in the sink and began to fill the pan with water from the tea kettle on the stove.

Later, theme music swirled into the room as the family sat on the couch a few feet from the radio. The announcer welcomed the listeners and added that tonight's episode was brought to them by Dreft. Music transitioned immediately to a commercial about Dreft laundry detergent.

"Do you think people buy that stuff just because they hear about it on these shows?" Michael wondered.

"Chet Bellum says women come in and ask for a product, mentioning that they heard about it on their wireless. The ads are convincing, and that is what pays for airing the programs. Some people are easily swayed." Mom smiled as she watched her son, amazed at his thinking.

Lydi hoped this show would make them laugh, but the chapter was a serious one. The little boy in the episode missed his older brother, who had gone to camp. Lydi worried that her own brother would lapse again to sadness. The keynote organ blared the conclusion of the show and the announcer touted the benefits of Dreft soap.

Michael listened intently, then turned to his mom. "We should buy some of that."

CHAPTER 40

SWEET RATIONS

Ethel Bollinger unlocked the cabinet that held the ration books and withdrew the packet of instructions and forms that required signatures and filing for government records. As the township teacher, she was responsible for administering the ration coupons the first Saturday of each month. Every man, woman and child, no matter what age, qualified for a ration book.

She glanced through the stamps before she tucked the books safely in the top drawer. This month's ration stamps included meat, coffee, butter and canned goods. Mileage stamps for gasoline covered the last page. There were three extra stamps for sugar and a form that needed to be signed by the recipient, promising that the sugar would be used for canning.

The majority of the residents accepted rationing as their contribution to the war effort. The American soldiers needed food and weapons. Most people willingly cut back, did without, or made do with what they had so there would be enough supplies for the men in combat, but there were always a few who complained that they did not get enough coupons.

After a quick peek at her watch pin, Ethel unlocked the schoolhouse door and returned to her desk. Immediately voices echoed from the front room and soon a young woman carrying a tiny infant ambled into the school room. A little boy skipped by her side, chattering noisily. The mother sat on one of the chairs lined in front of the teacher's desk. The child plopped into the front student desk behind his mother and opened the top to snoop inside. The cover slammed down as he moved to the next one.

Ethel quickly took four coupon packets from her drawer and set two forms out for the lady to sign, explaining about the extra sugar. The word drew the little boy's attention. "Sugar!" he repeated. "We don't need no more sugar. We got sugar stuffed in the couch and sugar under the bed."

With a sheepish smile, his mother rushed to place the ration coupons in her purse and sign the papers. She stood and reached out her hand to her son. After trying out the last desk in the row he skipped to his mother. "Are you gonna bake a cake today? I want chocolate with lots of chocolate frosting. And cherry Kool Aid to go with it." Ethel released a sigh of relief when the front door shut behind them and an older woman softly padded into the room.

Four hours later, rationing duties complete for another month, she headed outside to untie School

Boy Bill's reigns from the hitching post, and they rode to Canterbury.

"Good Day, Miss Bollinger." Chet nodded a smile as Ethel entered his store that also served as post office. "I see you have brought the ration forms from today. I will get them sent in right away. I have some papers to send to the office in Council Bluffs, too." He scratched the top of his bare head, then remembered. "Oh, you have some mail." He peered at the letter through his wire-rimmed spectacles. "Postmarked 'Oak Creek, Colorado.'"

Ethel grinned as she slipped her cousin's letter into her pocket book. Just in time to share with Mother and Esther as they enjoyed their Saturday afternoon coffee.

Billie's daycare business for the mothers who had gone to work in the nearby war materials factory was thriving. She enjoyed working with the children and every week they performed a short play or concert for the proud mothers. "They need something happy in their lives," Billie wrote, "something besides worry that they will lose their husbands."

Billie wrote about her friends who had been taken to the Japanese Internment Camp at Granada, Colorado. The buildings were all completed, including a school and store. No more prisoners had been brought in since February. Akito loved school at the camp and her family had adjusted to life there. Her father and other members of the camp council planned huge gardens where the residents would raise vegetables this summer. Some of the older people at the camp grew weak from not eating. They refused to eat the bread and cakes made with white flour when their whole lives they had eaten rice instead. Mr. Mori requested rice each time he met with government officials, but when weekly deliveries arrived, storeroom stacks grew taller, stacks of white flour and sugar.

Every letter from their cousin included at least a paragraph about how much she hated war and how unfair it was that the Japanese immigrants had to be imprisoned. She always had choice words for the leaders who involved our country and how ridiculous it was to fight each other like children. This letter she concluded with the same question that invaded their thoughts every day, "Will this war ever end?"

CHAPTER 41

GOLD STAR

"Mom, do you think Dad would have volunteered to fight in the war if he were alive?" Michael asked. The old truck lurched as Anna Andersson unconsciously lifted her foot from the gas pedal, taken aback by the question. A twinge of guilt twisted her heart as she realized she had never considered what her son was asking. Nearly four years had passed since she lost her husband, and though she thought of him every day, her thoughts had changed from sad longings to acceptance.

Golden heads of wheat bowed together gently in the wind, creating waves that raced the truck to the end of the field. The boy turned to his mother expectantly, waiting for an answer. Finally, she recovered and drew in a deep breath. "Yes, Michael. Your father would have been one of the first to join; I am certain of it." She reached over to touch her son's shoulder and managed a smile, though her voice caught as she went on. "He would have looked at you and Lydi and felt that he needed to protect you from Hitler's evils." She maneuvered the vehicle around a pothole in the rough gravel road. "He wanted us to be free."

The edge of Canterbury crept into view. Lydi glanced at her mother and tried to lighten the cloud of doom that hovered around them. "Are you going to Arden's house today?" She questioned her little brother, changing the subject abruptly. The three had begun the practice of driving to town every Saturday and spending several hours with families of soldiers.

Michael lifted the small box in his lap. "Yeah, I brought in my farm animals. All his toys are soldiers and tanks. I told him we need to play farm sometimes." Lydi caught a tiny smile on her mother's face as she focused on the road. Michael continued, "Then I am going to stop at Sena's. I told her I would help her pick tomatoes."

Lydi and Anna voiced their plans for the afternoon, and they decided to stop at the library first, and then make their visits. Michael stared out the window as houses passed in and out of view. Suddenly, his head turned and he stared back through the rear window. "Hey, Sena's got a gold star on her flag. Did you see it shining in her window?"

Anna swerved sharply to the right, off the road, and slammed down the brake. The children reached for the dash as they were propelled forward. The woman stared at her son. "What did you say, Michael?"

He frowned in confusion and shook his head, questioning the shock on his mother's face. "The star in her window. There used to be a red one. Now there is a gold one."

"Oh, no." Anna whispered and bowed her head, almost touching the steering wheel. When she looked up, her eyes were flooded with tears. She could tell that Lydi knew what the gold star meant, but she needed to prepare Michael.

Fifteen minutes later, Michael, Lydi and Anna knocked gently on Sena Gullickson's front door. They heard her call, not far from the entrance, her voice a hoarse rasp. "Come in. I'm here."

The old woman sat in her rocking chair. Her apron overflowed with bundles of envelopes that were tied together with string. She clutched a crisp paper with both hands. The family stood next to her, wishing to ease the pain they knew she felt. She spoke quietly, but her eyes fixated on the shelf on the wall before her, the shelf that held a picture of a young man in uniform and a model ship. "He was going to come home for Christmas, that grandson of mine." The chair rocked back and forth, the top of tan parchment in her hands bending with each movement. "WESTERN UNION" flashed across the top in bold black letters. Two small red stars stood out under the insignia. Lydi's eyes were drawn to the telegram. THE NAVY DEPARTMENT DEEPLY REGRETS TO INFORM YOU THAT YOUR GRANDSON LEVI GULLICKSON (SERGEANT FIRST CLASS) WAS KILLED IN ACTION IN THE PERFORMANCE OF HIS DUTY AND IN THE SERVICE OF HIS COUNTRY....

The chair creaked in continuous rhythm. Back and forth. Still, she stared at the shelf.

The visitors quietly moved chairs to gather at her side. They listened in silence.

"He wrote a while back that if he was the first to go he would prepare a place for me in heaven.

Heaven must have a baseball team, he said, and he was going to practice and get so good I will be proud of him when I get there." Then her head fell and she dropped the telegram as her hands covered her face. Her body shook violently and tears seeped from under her wrinkled hands. "But I always have been proud of him. Didn't he know that?"

For the first time she looked at the people next to her. The rocking stopped. Anna reached for the woman's hand, and the tears from their hands mingled in sadness. "Of course, he knew you were proud." Anna tried to be strong. She tried to hold back the sobs, but she could not.

Arms around her shaking shoulders, hands entwined, the three cried with Sena. They groped for something to say that might bring her some small fragment of comfort, but the words seemed empty and useless, so they just sat and listened as she spoke. She remembered times when the boy was growing up, how the two of them listened to every baseball game on the radio. His favorite pitcher. How he teased her when her number one batter struck out. She told her grandson she knew her player was as handsome as a movie star and Levi had laughed brightly.

The hours stole away that Saturday afternoon when Sena replaced her bright red star with the gold. At last the rocker resumed its cadence. She silently folded the telegram and placed it in its pouch. Her lips turned up wistfully as she wrapped her hands around the stacks of tattered envelopes that rested on her apron and lifted them to her heart. Her eyes turned back to the shelf on the wall, the picture. She breathed softly as one more tear slipped down her cheek. "At least I have his letters."

CHAPTER 42

LETTERS!

"How come Lydi gets all the mail?" Michael sulked as he handed his sister two letters. Lydi tolerantly patted his shoulder.

"Maybe if you would write letters you would get some in return," the young woman teased. Every letter lightened the dark cloud of worry that loomed over her, for it meant that Benjamin was alive and well.

Since he had left for training at Fort Lewis in Tacoma over six months ago, then later shipped to Italy, he had written. Some letters were short. Lydi understood that locations and battle plans needed to be kept secret, but she longed to know where he was and how much danger he faced. She knew he was part of a medical unit. Though he was still learning, his outfit was already active on the battle field. Benjamin wrote that the goal of the medical attachments was to conserve fighting strength. From the onset of training, their importance in winning the war had been drilled into them.

In his last letters, Ben talked of people. At the hospital in Naples, a Major Millern, a doctor from Omaha, Nebraska, instructed the soldiers, preparing them to function effectively in even the most severe conditions. Casualties filled the hospital to capacity. The most serious issue now was the morale of the men. The war had continued so long that many had given up hope of going home.

A seventeen-year-old from near Minot, North Dakota, enlisted at the same time as Ben. So far, their training and assignments matched exactly. Hermie Koehler grew up on a dairy farm and had never been away from home. Ben befriended the youngster when he noticed the boy withdrawing from the other recruits. The more intense the training became, the more horrendous the wound scenarios, the more depressed Hermie became. Benjamin worried about his friend, and wondered how he will hold up working in the heat of battle.

Later that day when Lydi and Anna stopped at the newspaper office to meet with Lynn and Becky, the women shared news of their men at war. Becky remembered her own bout with depression and prayed that the other women would not succumb to such melancholy.

"Have you heard from Brad?" Anna inquired of Lynn.

"Oh, yes, I get letters," she sighed wistfully, "but I can tell he is holding something back. Can't wait until he comes home." She turned to Lydi with a playful smile. "And how many letters do you get from your Benjamin?"

Lydi blushed and looked down. "I get one almost every day," she answered softly.

Lynn shook her head. "Oh, that young man is smitten!"

CHAPTER 43

BATTLES CONTINUE

Shaking his head sadly, Geoffrey sighed as he placed another red marker on the world map tacked to the wall behind the radio. He and William had been following the battles as they listened to nightly radio broadcasts and as they read daily headlines in the *Des Moines Register*. Geoffrey had cut tiny flags out of red and blue paper. After reports of each battle, he pinned the flags onto the map. Blue flags indicated victories and red, defeats. "We were doing jolly well there for a while," he said as he studied the pattern of colors and attached three more red banners. "But since the beginning of the year it seems the enemy's strength is insurmountable. What can we do, my dear brother?"

William's eyes narrowed in thought as he stared at his brother and the map. At last he gave a resolute nod. "We must continue to do what we have been. Tomorrow after chores, we can scour the countryside for more scrap metal."

"I will visit Mrs. Evans at the Doctor's office and inquire if her husband has need of more bandages." Geoffrey added, feeling a bit lighter knowing they were doing something to help. Christina peered into the living room just then.

"Tea is ready, gentlemen," she invited with a smile that belied her concern for the men. The older woman knew her husband and brother agonized over the war, how the enemy had destroyed so much of their mother country, especially the city of London, and how the battles kept droning on.

The Earl Grey and flaky crumpets Christina had made that morning could not chase away the sense of foreboding that loomed over Geoffrey as he sat in deep thought. How much longer could the country continue to fight? How many more young lives would be lost?

CHAPTER 44

MAYBE

Lydi turned from the stove expectantly as Michael brought the mail into the kitchen. The boy frowned slightly as he tossed the papers onto the table. He knew his sister was missing the usual letters from Benjamin. "Sorry, Lydi," he said kindly. "No letters today, but I bet there will be one on Monday."

The young woman swallowed the lump that rose in her throat and stared at the pile of mail. Since Benjamin had joined the army eight months ago, never had she gone more than four days without receiving a letter. Sometimes it was just a short note. Sometimes he wrote about training, the other men in his troop, and the people in the towns. She had counted on his letters. This time, ten days elapsed and still no letter. Each day she counted off loomed over her. The days crawled by, minute by minute, and every minute the image of her dear friend flashed through her mind.

In the last letter she had received, he had written that his unit would be moving, going into battle. Maybe it took more time for the letters to reach the mail stations. The young friend from North Dakota who enlisted the same time had been distraught and homesick. Maybe Ben was spending extra time helping Hermie deal with his fears.

Then deep, dark thoughts seeped into her heart. What if he had been hurt? What if the Germans had captured him? The image of Sena with the Western Union telegram in her trembling hands slammed into Lydi's brain. What if Benjamin had been killed?

CHAPTER 45

PROMISES REMEMBERED

Lynn was standing on a metal step-stool, bent over the side of the hulking printing press when Lydi walked into the door of the newspaper office. The woman looked up and flashed a bright smile at her young friend. "Hey, Lydi!" Lynn called as she stepped down, a streak of black ink smudged on her nose. "How are things going?" she inquired, pulling back a chair next to the front table and gestured for Lydi to do the same.

Lydi sat, her hands folded on the table in front of her, and quietly gazed at the stack of last week's edition of the *Canterbury Times-News*.

Lynn watched her young friend for a few moments, then leaned forward. "Lydi, something is wrong. What is it?"

Releasing a huge sigh, Lydi poured out her worries. More than three weeks had elapsed since she had received a letter from Ben. She reported what he had written about his lonely friend, where they had trained and that his company was ready for battle.

Lynn reached to place her right hand on Lydi's. "I know you are worried, Lydi. That is what we do, but there could be many reasons no letters are coming. I went for more than two weeks with not a letter from Brad, only to learn that the bag of mail had been lost. One day there were seven letters, all written weeks ago."

Tears threatened, but Lydi managed to meet the woman's eyes. "I know. I tell myself all those things, but then I think of the grandson that Sena lost. I hear the news on the radio, and the list of fallen soldiers, and the fear starts all over again."

Lynn stood and walked around the table to wrap an arm around the girl. "Hope for the future keeps us going from day to day. You must not give up, Lydi."

Her heart felt lighter as she closed the door of the newspaper office behind her and started on the boardwalk to the edge of town. Lynn's empathetic words had reminded Lydi of the promises the family had made to her dad when he was dying, that they would never give up, no matter what. A pang of guilt elbowed in as she realized she had not recalled those promises for months. The reminder, like a sign, sparked hope inside her.

As she neared Sena Gullickson's small house where Michael had spent the afternoon, she heard voices in the back yard. A soft murmur barely reached her, something about missing him so much. She heard her little brother's unabashed advice.

"But he wouldn't want you to be sad all the time. He'd want you to go on living."

Just as she was about to turn the corner, Lydi heard Michael's final message, loud and clear. "You can't give up, Sena, not ever."

CHAPTER 46

NEWS

"Lydi! Lydi! You have company!" Michael called from the bottom of the stairs. "It's Ben's mom and dad. And Adam."

On the first step down, Lydi stopped short. Ben's parents? Why would they come to the farm to see her? They must have news about Benjamin. Relief and worry warred inside her as she hurried downstairs and to the front door.

Christina was already outside on the porch, and she reached for her daughter as the girl stepped outside. The mother put her arm around her shoulders as if to brace her for what was to come. Adam Hindricks stood, grimly waiting for his parents, as his father opened the car door for his wife and offered her his arm. As they turned to the house, Lydi could see that the woman had been crying. New worry lines etched her face and she shook her head slowly. She clutched a slip of paper in her left hand. Even from the distance, Lydi could tell it was a telegram. Memories of Sena's telegram informing her of her son's death tore through Lydi and her heart pounded frantically. She should greet them, walk to them, but, dreading the news they brought, she stood like a statue, her body unwilling to cooperate with her brain.

Haltingly, the three approached Lydi. Phyllis Hindricks reached for the girl and pulled her into her arms as she began to sob. "He's alive, Lydi. Ben is alive."

Relieved, Lydi hugged Benjamin's mother, then stepped back to look into her eyes. Through the tears, Lydi saw worry and sorrow and something else. Fear. Lydi waited, unwilling to ask, but screaming inside. *What else? What other news do you have?*

Benjamin's father stepped forward and reached for the young woman's arm. "He has been injured, Lydi. Right now he is hospitalized somewhere in Italy." His wife wavered, hearing his words and Adam immediately moved next to her. "We do not know the extent of his injuries, only that they are serious."

Lydi nodded. Weeks of worry had grown and festered inside her, and she suddenly realized she had selfishly turned inward, as if unable to bear any more pain. When she should have been reaching out to Ben's family, she had focused only on her own despair.

His voice caught with emotion as the father added, "He was trying to save a friend."

Lydi's pent-up tears flowed as she hugged Benjamin's mother, father and brother. A thoughtful smile turned her lips slightly. "That is so like Benjamin. You raised a good man."

Now Ben's family remained silent as Lydi stood before them, praying for wisdom, for strength, for words. Praying for all of them.

"He is alive." She straightened her spine and drew in a steadying breath. "There is hope." Then, a ray of courage coursed through her and she reached for Phyllis' hands. "We must not give up."

CHAPTER 47

TURNABOUT

Geoffrey grinned as he pinned three more blue "victory" flags on the map, indicating more successful Allied battles. "Dresden will put us over the edge, William, indubitably." He glanced at his brother who sat in his rocker, the *Des Moines Register* open before him.

William nodded in agreement. Last month the two brothers had scoured the countryside, coming up with another truckload of metal for the salvage center. With the positive turnabout in Europe, the two finally dared to hope that their relentless home front support of the war made a difference. "Yes, I agree we are now in a positive stronghold, but with dire consequences. There is no more room for the injured in the military hospitals." Both men's thoughts turned to Lydi's Benjamin, but neither voiced their worries.

Geoffrey stared at the flag covered map. "If only Japan would yield in their fanatic view of war. I fear much more blood will be shed before they give in."

CHAPTER 48

THREE WORDS

Lydi's hands shook as she clutched the thin letter in her hands. Ben's return address was scrawled in the left-hand corner. It had been four months since she had received a letter from him. Nearly two months since his parents had brought the telegram about his injury. She wanted to tear the letter open and see the words in the handwriting of her beloved. But she was afraid.

Finally, she retreated to the quiet of her own room and eased slowly down to the edge of her bed. She prayed for strength. She prayed that the news would be good news. After carefully lifting the flap on the back of the envelope, the young woman removed the single sheet of white paper. Heart beating wildly, she unfolded it and stared at Ben's handwriting.

"I'm coming home!"

CHAPTER 49

WAITING

The three women sat around the front table in the office of the *Canterbury Times-News*. Every week they met under pretense of gathering ideas for newspaper stories, but each knew the real reason for their talks; they shared the common bond of waiting for their loved one to come home.

"Paul thinks the war will be over soon," Becky Evans smiled hopefully at her companions. "But he said even if it isn't, he is coming home for Christmas." Her friends understood her excitement. Somehow in the last few months, their thoughts had changed from "if the war ever ends" to "when they come home." Could it be possible, or was it just wishful thinking because they could no longer bear the worries or the fear that their men would not come home? She added quietly, "Mary Ann will remember her daddy, but Mack will not. He is too little."

Lydi listened and prayed that all would be fine with Becky and their family. The young mom seemed to have overcome the severe depression that had haunted her. Lydi's thoughts returned to Ben and she prayed that he would be home soon. That he would heal, no matter how severe his wounds.

Lynn shook her head pensively. "It seems all the men are dreaming of coming home. It is amazing how their plans have changed in the last few months. Grace Feldman said her husband wrote that when he comes home, they are going to buy a farm. He wants his family to live in the peace of the country."

Then she laughed softly and rolled her eyes upward. "And get this! Brad, my dear husband, Brad.

You, know, the guy who headed off to war with his camera in his hand? The man who was going to document it all in words and pictures? In his last letter he informed me that all his pictures are the property of the U.S. government. He cannot bring home one roll of film, not even one picture. He says everything he has worked on is privileged information, and when he comes home he will not even be able to tell me what he has done." She slapped both hands down on the table in frustration. "The reporter who cannot report!"

The other two did not know how to reply, but they had learned in their support sessions that words were not always necessary, so they waited.

Pent-up tears flooded Lynn's eyes and she looked down at her ink-stained hands. "I only hope that what he is doing over there makes a difference. I hope that he is helping win this dreadful war."

CHAPTER 50

BRAD'S UNWRITTEN REPORT

I just hope this will help win the war. Bradley Swanson thought to himself as he waited for his pilot and friend to emerge from the massive doors at Bletchley Park. Brad's photos, taken while the small plane deftly swooped over enemy ports and camps, had been delivered to the Command Station in London. Following each flight Fred unfailingly drove the eight miles to Bletchley Park, the huge mansion where his girlfriend worked as a codebreaker.

Today, the daring pilot's smile rivaled the sun as he trotted to the car, opened the driver's door and crawled in. "Well, mate, I think we did it! Your ace photos helped the chaps at Command match up the messages in the Germans' code. Our B-17s will make quick work of those ships. We're winning, Old Boy. Lucy cannot reveal details, but she says it is just a matter of time."

Brad nodded a grin at his friend. "You helped a little, you know. I could not have flown Maude. "

Fred tipped back his head and hooted a whole-hearted laugh. He slapped Brad's shoulder. "Yes, Mate, we did it together, and I'm right chuffed we did it. You will soon be going home to take pictures of cornfields and cows."

Brad chuckled softly at the Englishman's view of his newspaper life in America. He shook his head as he thought of how he would explain his part in the war to Lynn. Privileged information. That meant he could tell no one, not even his dear wife. Would he ever be able to share the stories with her? Would their children know how their father's photographs had been used in the war effort? He longed to write down the whole story. The flights made under the cover of darkness. The German fighters that had spotted them and fired. The sound of bullets pelleting the side of the Mosquito as it dove down through a cloud of mist, then flitted to safety on the Allied side. The photos he hoped were clear in spite of the vibration of Maude's engines. The code-breakers, hundreds of women who worked relentlessly to break German and Japanese code messages. What a story he could write, but no, not this time, not this story.

The two men rode back to the air base in silence, each lost in his own thoughts. Brad shook his head slowly. *At least I will be going home soon. That is what really matters.*

CHAPTER 51

SCARS

Lydi glanced in the clouded mirror above her dresser. Would Benjamin like what he saw? Would he remember her as she looked before he had left for war? She knew she had changed, inside and out. Then her thoughts turned back to the worries that had haunted her for the last four months. Why had he not written? Were his injuries so severe that he could not write? Not remember? Horrible scenes flashed through her mind until she chided herself for the foolish torture. *He is home.*

Adam, Benjamin's little brother, had walked over the night before to let Lydi know Ben had arrived home that day. With a silly grin, he informed her that he was pretty sure Ben would be over to see

Lydi "real soon." A bud of hope sprung up in her heart and started to bloom as she waited, pushing away her fears.

The soft engine sound of the the Hindricks' Zephyr flitted through the living room window, followed by the gentle closing of a car door. Unable to wait any longer, the young woman rushed through the front door and onto the outside porch. The man strode toward her. His bright smile flashed, but then faded slightly. His pace slowed as he grew near the girl he had grown to love, the one he hoped would share his life. Five feet from the steps he stopped. He studied her face. "Lydi." He spoke softly.

"Oh, Ben!" she cried and ran to him. She threw her arms around his neck and hugged him, tears streaming onto his white shirt. At last she pulled away and put her hands on his arms. She looked up at him. Again, he watched for her reaction, a wince, or a head turn of revulsion like those of the nurses and the other soldiers.

She reached up to touch his face and smiled at him. "Are you all right, Benjamin?" He nodded slightly while wondering if her fingers would feel the disfigurement. "I have missed you so much." Then, though she had promised she would not ask, at least not today, the words blurted out. "Why did you not write, Ben?"

The young man heaved a deep sigh. "I was scared, Lydi. I didn't know if you would want me anymore."

Her brows creased in a frown and she stared at him incredulously. "Why would you think such a thing?"

He chuckled softly, and wondered if he dare hope. Then he took her hand and gently settled it on the side of his face. She felt it then, the roughness, the scars. She turned his head so she could see them and lovingly stroked the jagged red marks. Like a caress, she softly brushed the branded skin, running her fingers from his face down to his shirt collar.

"Oh, Ben," she breathed, but there was only compassion in her glistening eyes. She drew him back to her and rested her head next to his heart. At last, realization of his words dawned on her and she looked up into his eyes. "You thought I would not love you because you have scars?"

He looked away foolishly. "Well, the nurses avoided me after they saw my face. Some of the guys said their girlfriends didn't want to marry them after they were injured. It broke their hearts." He felt guilty now, for doubting her, but he had thought he needed to give her the chance to back out if that was what she wanted. "I figured if I did not write, you might give up on me and it would not hurt so much if we...parted. That maybe it would be easier for you."

Lydi stepped back then and put her hands on her hips. "Benjamin Franklin Hindricks, do you think I am so shallow that a couple scars would end my love for you?" He grinned, thinking how she had changed. What happened to the shy girl she had been before he left?

Then her voice softened and she reached for his hand. "Can you tell me what happened, Ben? What horrible things have you experienced?"

He shrugged nonchalantly. He breathed in, then released a huge sigh as he remembered. Finally, he answered. "Well, Hermie decided he didn't think life was worth living anymore. I just let him know I begged to differ."

CHAPTER 52

AUGUST 14, 1945

Lydi leaned her head into Ginger's hip as she brought forth the Jersey cow's rich milk into the bucket before her. The young woman's hands continued to work as her mind wandered. She thought of Benjamin. It was so good to have him back. Maybe the other soldiers would come home soon. Surely, Japan would surrender now after two of their cities had been devastated by atomic bombs. Japan had become even more deadly when faced with defeat and doggedly refused any discussion of peace. President Truman, hoping to bring a quick end to the war, had given the order for American B-52 bombers to drop bombs on Hiroshima and Nagasaki. Thousands of people had been killed. How long would Japan stubbornly continue to fight? Lydi stripped the last milk from the gentle cow and tossed a flake of hay into her trough.

Chores finished, Lydi and Michael strolled to the house where Mom would have supper waiting for them. Michael's stomach growled. "I wonder what Mom made for supper tonight. I'm starved!" Lydi smiled. It was no wonder her little brother was not so little anymore; most of his thoughts dealt with food.

Suddenly they stopped. What was that noise? The August breeze carried the sound of bells ringing wildly from town. Their eyes met before they tore to the house.

"Mom! Mom!" Michael cried. "Something must have happened. The church bells in Canterbury are ringing nonstop!"

"Oh!" Anna breathed. "The war. Could it be?" They rushed to the living room and turned on the radio. The announcer shouted above the din of

251

shouting and fireworks. "The war is over! The Japanese surrendered today, five days after the second atomic bomb was dropped over Japan. Stay tuned for President Truman's announcement…"

CHAPTER 53

THE NEXT DAY AT SCHOOL

Lydi rushed into the school room to see Ethel. They hugged as happy tears streamed from their faces. At last the war was over. Outside they heard noises of children on the playground. Little girls shrieked wildly from the Merry-Go-Round as someone must have given it a push. There came a crack of bat hitting ball and boys yelled to the runner. "Home run! Home run!"

"It is so good to hear happy playground noises again. I hate to end it." Ethel smiled at Lydi as they walked to the school porch where Ethel rang the bell.

"Awww, already?" could be heard among groans of protest at having playtime ended, but the youngsters filed into the school.

Lydi sat in the desk next to Emma, the only Svenson girl still attending school. "The sisters said to tell you hello," Emma smiled over at Lydi. "Ida is getting married to Oscar. Mabel has a beau. His name is Harrison," she added with a dramatic sigh. "It is SO romantic," she breathed, as her gaze drifted to the boys' side of the room. Then she glanced back at Lydi. "Julia and Lilly still help with chores sometimes, but they are working for a couple neighbors. And Ma is anxious to have Elmer and Art home."

Lydi's thoughts turned to Benjamin. It seemed strange that life could change so quickly. She looked around the one-room classroom. Arden Feldman sidled next to Michael, gazing up at him with adoring eyes. Ricky Christleton, feet swaying forward and back in turn, sat next to Arden.

Vicky Christleton whispered to little Amelia Feldman. The young twin had taken paper and crayons from her desk immediately after "The Pledge of Allegiance" and begun drawing. Lydi watched as the creation emerged. There were people, adults holding the hands of children, many children. At last Vicky reached for her red crayon. On each person she drew a wide smile that covered their whole face.

At the end of the day, Ethel dismissed her students and watched them dash out of the classroom, calling to friends. Lydi stayed for a few minutes and the two friends talked. They spoke of Benjamin and his work at the medical school in Omaha with soldiers who suffered from shellshock. Of how Lydi would soon join him at college.

They walked together to the front steps. Lydi thought she noticed a sparkle in her friend's eyes. Ethel smiled and said, "Life is so different now."

Lydi nodded and began her half mile walk home, thinking how good it would be to see Ben that weekend, how happy he would be that the war was over. Less than a hundred yards down the road, the young woman heard a vehicle driving into the school yard. She stopped and turned around to watch. A shiny maroon Chevy Coupe pulled up to the front steps. The driver got out of the car, a young man with dark hair. Ethel stood on the top step waiting, her face beaming with a warm, happy smile.

CHAPTER 54

BASEBALL, SHEEP AND CHOCOLATE CHIP COOKIES

Sena Gullickson woke up early that Saturday morning. Michael and Arden were coming as they did nearly every Saturday. She mixed the dough for her special chocolate chip cookies. The boys loved them. Levi had loved them, too. She thought wistfully of her grandson who had been killed in Italy, leading his troops into battle. Sadness and loss threatened to overtake her.

Then she thought of Levi's promise that he would save a place for her, and practice on Jesus' baseball team. The picture warmed her heart as she slid a pan of cookie dough into the oven. Levi had loved baseball. She missed him terribly, but she knew she had to go on. The two young boys who had come into her life after Levi died filled some of the empty places in her heart.

Today they would listen to the last game of the World Series on her old radio. The Detroit Tigers were playing the Chicago Cubs. The old woman smiled in anticipation of the boys' antics as the game was played, the jumping and cheering, groaning over an umpire's call. She found herself looking forward to the afternoon.

There was a polite knock on the back door, quickly followed by two youngsters bounding in. "Hi, Sena! You ready for the game? It smells good in here!"

Little Arden fidgeted with pent-up excitement. "Today is the best day, ever, Sena! We're gonna listen to the game and eat cookies. Then Michael and I are going back to his house 'cause his sheep had triplets. Dad said maybe I could buy a sheep and start my own flock, just like Michael. I love livin' on a farm."

Sena noted the sparkle in the young boy's eyes and remembered days long ago when Levi was young. She nodded her head slowly and smiled.

CHAPTER 55

BRAD'S MEMORIES AND PLANS

Brad held Lynn's hand as they took a Sunday drive through the country, winding around Iowa fields and farms. His wife's eyes sparkled with happiness. Her man had been home nearly two months!

"I've been thinking maybe I can do a piece on the Iowa farmer. Bet *Look* magazine would like to run something calm like that after all the war stories." His face turned serious at the mention of war.

They pulled into a short drive at the end of a vast cornfield. The stalks and leaves had turned brown and full ears protruded, brown silks shrinking to reveal golden kernels on top, ready for harvest. The two exited the car and stood, taking in the fresh country air, the peaceful scene. Suddenly the drone of an airplane could be heard approaching. Brad looked up and stared. Lynn heard him mumble something that sounded like a woman's name. "Maude?" There was a questioning look in her eyes.

Brad chuckled and gave her neck a gentle massage. "Maude was Fred's plane."

Lynn knew Brad would speak no more of the flights, the missions. Today she did not mind, for she was quite certain that she had a new secret that could top his any day. Hope of a tiny new life warmed her heart and her hand rested softly on her stomach.

At last the reporter turned back. He focused on the corn.

CHAPTER 56

BILLIE'S CHANGE OF HEART

Dear Ethel, Lydi and all,

I am so thankful that the war is over! Maybe our lives will get back to "normal." Ethel, your young students will be happier now. School will take on a whole new focus, as will our lives. Your letters about how much the little ones worried about the future tore at my heart.

Lydi, I can only imagine how happy you are to have Benjamin back. Soon you will join him at medical school. I cannot help but smile thinking of calling you "Doctor Andersson" someday. Your last year of school at Canterbury will fly by quickly.

My friend Akito and her family must remain in the Japanese internment camp for a few more months. They always impressed me for their ability to take life in stride and go on. Being removed from their homes and jobs did not seem to faze them. Akito wrote that their camp raised enough vegetables for all of the camps in the country. Though she did not boast, I believe her father provided the leadership for the gardens as well as other camp activities.

I cannot wait to see Akito. How much will she have changed in these four years? I still have her possessions stashed under my bed, the things she could not take with her when they were forced to leave their home.

Dru no longer works at the factory in Boulder. Of course, the war materials are not needed anymore, so it has been converted back to its pre-war business. The government issued orders that men, especially returning soldiers, are to have first priority for all factory jobs. More and more men arrive on the trains every day.

Only two children remain in my day care business, and their mothers will likely be released from their jobs in the next month or so. It has been a good experience. I guess I feel that I may have contributed in a small way to the war effort on the home front.

Speaking of the home front, I have exciting news! Four weeks ago as I was walking home with arms loaded with blankets the day care children used for a theater, a man stood from his bench at the train depot and approached me. None of Mother's admonitions about talking to strangers came to mind this time. For some reason this man did not seem like a stranger. He was in uniform, on leave. He asked if he could help carry my parcels. On the walk home I learned that he was visiting family near Oak Creek. He is on furlough from the Air Force, Airman First Class.

Since that Sunday, he has come back to see me every weekend. He will soon leave for George Air

Force Base in California, but he promised to write as soon as he gets there. He will, I can feel it in my heart.

Yes, my heart does flip-flops when I think of him. He is kind, smart and handsome. His name is Don. Do you think I would be a good military wife?

My love to all of you.

> *Your Cousin and Friend,*
>
> *Billie*

CHAPTER 57

BROTHERS

Benjamin met William and Geoffrey at the front door of the new treatment facility for soldiers. Dr. Elijah Millern had spearheaded the center when he returned from his stint in an American war hospital in Italy. Millern had trained Ben, been impressed with his innate medical aptitude, and invited him to begin study at the Omaha Medical College, where Millern taught.

Benjamin had grown to love the two old gents as much as Lydi. He invited them to visit the disturbed soldiers. They did, and then returned every Monday morning. "Thank you, Geoffrey and William, for coming here to visit these men."

Dr. Millern met them in the hall and shook hands with the older men. "It is good of you to come, Geoffrey. William. There are three more patients since your last visit. One of the men is extremely disturbed. We cannot seem to reach him. He has not spoken one word since he arrived at our facility. The man just stares at the ceiling." The doctor's eyes radiated compassion for the man who suffered such mental anguish. "We know only that he was a pilot. He was shot down over Germany and taken prisoner, and none of the other men in his group survived."

Geoffrey shook his head sadly, staring down at his folded hands. "In what room may I find this man?"

William, Benjamin and Dr. Millern left Geoffrey with Captain John Winter. As they started down the hall, they heard Geoffrey's gentle voice. "I was naïve enough to believe that I could serve my country as a pilot. They refused my enlistment. I was too old, they said. I was angry...."

"I hope Geoffrey will not be too discouraged if he cannot reach that man." The doctor shook his head sadly. "The best psychiatrists in D.C. tried and failed."

William inclined his head slightly, as though listening to something from afar. His eyes met Benjamin's for a second, then he replied to the physician with a grin, "Possibly. You may be surprised, good doctor."

Two hours later, as the three again passed by the captain's room, they heard the broken words. The voice was raspy and soft. "....there were children and women....screaming....I can still hear it at night when I try to sleep. Then my men...tortured...." The fragments turned to sobs, heart-wrenching sobs that continued until William, Benjamin and the doctor were out of earshot.

On the ride home, William patted his brother on the back with a proud smile. "Dr. Millern and Ben said your visit with John today was nothing short of a miracle. You persuaded the young man to talk."

"Ah, hardly a miracle, Brother William. I was just continuing our battle on the home front."

CHAPTER 58

SELMA'S TWO-STARRED FLAG

She stopped short, wire basket of eggs swaying heavily from her left hand as she trudged from the chicken coop to the house. Out on the road, car doors slammed shut and Selma waited and stared at the rutted driveway that emerged from the copse of cottonwood and wild plums. Soon two men in olive green uniform emerged and trudged from the road toward the farm house. They scanned the property with tired eyes.

Suddenly the basket dropped to the ground. Selma ran to them as a silent prayer of thanks rose to heaven. *My boys! They are home!*

Arthur and Elmer Svenson dropped their bags next to the thin, dark wainscoting that paneled the bottom half of the kitchen wall. They sank wearily into high-backed chairs. With joyful tears streaming down her face, their mother hugged them again and again and fussed over them. "I did not know you were coming home."

"We thought we'd surprise you, Ma." Arthur tried to force a smile on his drawn face. "Elmer was in the hospital for a while after Normandy."

Selma gasped and stared at her son. "You were hurt? We did not know. Are you all right? What happened?"

Elmer tried to look his mother in the eyes, but his glance fell to the glass of spoons that rested in the center of the table in front of him. As long as he could remember, a clear glass tumbler had set on the table, loaded with teaspoons, ready to stir coffee or dip into ice cream. The sight of those spoons comforted him somehow. "I'm all right, Ma," he said quietly. She did not see the haunted look in his eyes.

Arthur sighed as he watched his brother. How could he explain to their mother? How could he tell her that Elmer had lain in his hospital bed for weeks after his torn shoulder had healed, but the doctors could find nothing physically wrong with him? How he spent daylight hours staring at the bare lightbulb above with empty eyes? How he screamed in the darkness when nightmares over-took him? How he would not speak of the horrors of that dreadful night at Normandy. Shellshock, the doctors called it.

"He just had to rest up, didn't you, Elmer?" Art patted his brother on the back. Elmer nodded slightly, still staring quietly at the spoons.

Selma took in the sight of the sons she had prayed for and worried about for so long. "I am so glad you are home." She turned to the stove and filled the coffeepot with fresh water, measured the coffee and set the vessel on the front burner. "You are so thin. We'll have to put some meat back on those bones." Her blue Swedish eyes crinkled at the edges that had grown deeper in the last years. She took a loaf of bread from the pantry, wishing she had baked that morning. There was ham in the ice box from last night's supper. She cut thick slices and plopped them onto buttered bread. *Ost,* she brought out the chunk of cheese Julia and Ida had made. The enticing aroma of Mabel's spice cake soon enveloped them. She cut two huge slabs. When a feast beckoned from the table, the mother cajoled. "Eat!"

At last Elmer's gaze lifted to his mother and he grinned. "Ja, Ma, but you don't have to fatten us up in one meal!" Her heart lightened at his playful rib. He would be all right. Her boys were home.

Late that night, when her family slept safely in their beds, Selma softly stole into the living room where, for nearly four years, the family Bible had rested beside the flag, the Mother's flag that her husband had brought home for her when her sons had gone off to war.

With her left hand resting on the Bible, she brushed her thin fingers softly over the flag's two blue hearts. Carefully she unfolded the red-framed banner and tears again threatened. She glanced to the front window that faced the road. Only the white glare of the lamp stared back at her. Suddenly her chin lifted with pride and a twinkle sparkled in her Swedish eyes. Resolutely, she strode to the kitchen and came back with the step-stool. She pulled the hinged bottom out next to the window and spritely ascended to the top. She lifted the curtain rod from its hooks and removed the white lace curtain.

Some time later, Selma Svenson turned off the lantern and crawled into bed next to her sleeping husband. Her heart whispered another prayer of thanks and she grinned into the darkness. The Bible still held its place of honor on the delicate doily on the lamp table, but the white flag, the Mother's flag with the wide red border and two bright blue stars hung proudly in the front window.

JOURNAL OF LYDI ANNA ANDERSSON

DECEMBER 15, 1945

Though the war seemed to drag on forever over the last four years, it still does not seem possible that I am now 18. So much happened during that time. Many things changed, and for some the changes were devastating. I cannot help but think of Sena and all those who lost loved ones. I admire them for plodding on.

It seems like the whole country was holding its breath, worrying about what was coming next, afraid to dream or laugh. Afraid to make promises, for fear they would be broken. Then the war was over and almost overnight, happiness returned.

People are getting married, starting families, beginning new jobs. The cloud of war scudded over us and is gone.

Christmas will be merry again. Grandma Christina is coming over next Saturday for Christmas baking. Michael has requested three more favorite cookies for us to bake. No more rationing! Becky and the children are thrilled that their husband and daddy will soon be home, hopefully this time for good.

In just a few months I will graduate high school from Canterbury Township 7. Ethel will continue to teach, at least for a while, but she will soon be Mrs. Ward. She will be marrying the handsome young farmer who has been courting her.

A year from now I will have begun classes at Omaha Medical College. It will be good to see Benjamin almost every day. He wants me to help with the treatment facility for soldiers who suffer from mental affliction from the war.

Ben speaks of marriage, though he says we must wait until he can support us while we both finish medical school. I cannot imagine spending my life with anyone but him, but do I dare dream?

Like the time, seven years ago, when our family rode the train to Iowa to fulfill our dreams, life is exciting and scary. We do not know what the future holds, but we must move toward it.

So, we make new promises. Still, I think the promise our family made to our Dad before he died needs to continue. This one promise should endure throughout our lives and the generations that follow—We must not give up, no matter what.

---Lydi Anna Andersson

ABOUT THE AUTHOR

Besides her five published books, *Promises to Keep, Promises Challenged, Promises Strengthened, Promises in Courage,* and *Promises Under Fire*, (available at Amazon.com), DeAnn Kruempel currently writes a column, NOOKS AND CRANNIES, that appears in three Midwest newspapers. Kruempel hopes to publish a compilation of the popular stories in the near future.

The author was born and raised on a farmnear De Smet, South Dakota. She has also lived in rural North Dakota and Iowa. For more than 30 years she has worked at school and public libraries. DeAnn is currently the Children's Librarian at the Missouri Valley Public Library.

The author enjoys working in her orchard, reading and spending time with family and friends. She lives on an acreage near Logan, Iowa with her cat, Elsa, 11,293 honeybees, four ducks and 17 chickens.

CREDITS and THANKS

I dedicate this book to everyone who has ever felt so alone and devastated that they questioned the value of this earthly life. May they find true peace.

To Little Black Banty, who died when this book was being written—thank you for inspiring yet another story.

Special thanks to Ethel, Billie, Neighbor Larry, Bill and Joetta and Lee for the stories.

To my siblings, children, grandchildren, friends, nieces, nephews and cousins---your support and encouragement are the most wonderful rewards I could ever receive. Thank you!

Thanks to my editors, Bruce and Dorothy, and to publisher Nathan at BookStudio.

To God, who always keeps His promises.

www.ingramcontent.com/pod-product-compliance
Lightning Source LLC
Chambersburg PA
CBHW051249260626
47162CB00002B/673